RESENTMENT

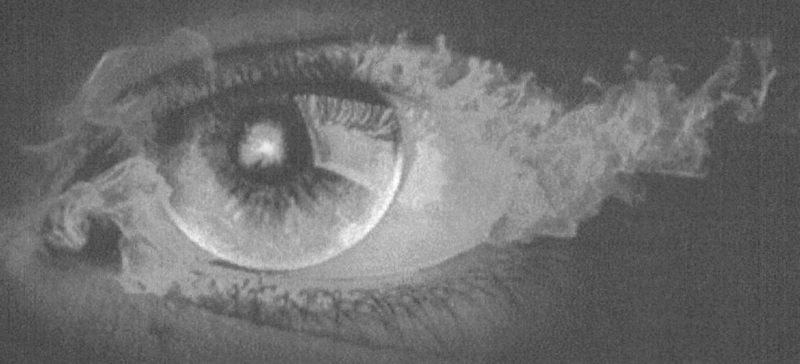

anthology

Indignor House
Fall 2022

anthology

RESENTMENT

ISBN 978-1-953278-33-3 Hard Back
ISBN 978-1-953278-34-0 Soft Back
ISBN 978-1-953278-35-7 E-Book

Published by

INDIGNOR HOUSE™

Virginia USA
www.IndignorHouse.com

Contents

Contents - Continued

An Introduction

There's something about life that's a mystery. Not sure if it stems from how we, as humans, relate to each other or how we, as humans, relate to the environment. Within either, there are things that definitely affects us.

We created Indignor House to promote the silent voices. Voices that, otherwise, are left unheard or unread. In today's realm of hostile social media and hateful, random postings, we must ask ourselves two simple questions.

Were the words spoken or written a paid announcement from a radical political group?

or ...

Were the words a personal truth from someone who was working through an emotional ordeal?

After digging deeper into either, we then must understand that what we just read or heard may take on a different meaning or concept. And ... it could be a realization that is quite painful to accept or acknowledge.

For our first short story competition, Indignor House chose the concept of *resentment,* and our authors did not disappoint us. Through their unique voices, the conceptualization of life took shape and became the stories that you are about to read. Our reality of what we experience and how we react may vary. However, at the same time, the truth our reality reflects demonstrates that we are all the same. And perhaps ...

what is written within these pages is a truth that we must accept and respect.

Jealousy, revenge, rejection, failure, resentment, envy … emotions that haunt even the most brave, the most tolerant, the most rich, or the most successful. Experiencing these emotions only prove that we must survive while constantly challenging what the world places before us. We can choose to walk around the obstacles or charge through them. Neither is an easy decision, and at times, it may be easier to simply give up and allow the environment to take over. Our authors, however, decided to not give in and to take charge. They guided their pens … and with an attitude, their stories were written.

Many years ago, my mother told me something about my sister, and how she hated her shoes. My father had bought her new ones, but she still was not happy.

"A hidden message is behind every action or non-action," my mother had said. "You must listen to everything to understand."

While working on my master's in literature, I had to write a story for a flash fiction class. Using my mother's wise words, *The Shoes* was created. This short story has been published numerous times and won two awards. Please enjoy.

For each of our submissions, I wanted to discuss what I believe was hidden between their lines. Let us see if you find the same hidden meanings that I did.

And we at Indignor House hope that from these kind words, we are able to pass on a little wisdom to explain why mankind reacts as it does.

Lynn Yvonne Moon
Chief Executive Officer

The Shoes

Lynn Yvonne Moon

The dishes rattled on the shelf as a pair of black shoes bounced off the cabinet.

"I HATE MY SHOES!"

A banging bedroom door, again, rattled the dishes.

"Why don't you buy the child a new pair of shoes?" the father asked.

"Because . . ." the mother replied, "it's not the shoes."

"It's obvious that the child doesn't like her shoes." Picking up the small pair, the father studied them. Nothing special, just black patent leather with a small nylon bow.

"It's not the shoes," the mother repeated.

"What else could it be?" The father glanced over at the empty hallway.

"It's not the shoes," the mother said again.

Staring out the window, the father watched as several young children ran down the sidewalk. They seemed happy. Why wasn't his daughter happy? Tonight, he would purchase her a new pair. Then, his wife's words echoed through his mind – *it's not the shoes*.

"It has to be the shoes," he whispered.

The following afternoon, a pair of bright red shoes flew through the air before bouncing twice on the sofa.

"I HATE MY SHOES!" The child's voice screeched through the father's ears.

"I just bought her those shoes last night and she loved them." Scratching his head, the father frowned.

"It's not the shoes," the mother said.

"If it's not the shoes, then what is it?"

Smiling, she replied, "Why don't you ask her?"

The father knocked before opening his daughter's door. "May I ask what's wrong with your new shoes, child?"

The little girl wiped her eyes. "I hate 'em!"

"Last night you said you loved them? What's really bothering you?"

The little girl stared at the shoes that were in her father's hands. "Jessica said my shoes are stupid and ugly and so am I." Wiping her nose with the back of her hand, she sighed.

"And who is Jessica?"

"A mean girl on the bus."

"Do you really hate these shoes?"

The child studied the shoes. "No ..."

"I see." He paused, adding, "Does Jessica wear pretty black or red shoes?"

"No."

"Is Jessica nice to you?"

"No."

"Then is Jessica worth listening to?"

The child stared at her father and smiled. "No."

"Do you like your shoes?"

Nodding, she replied, "Yes."

"Then it's not the shoes."

Lynn Yvonne Moon

The Shoes

Nick Tseffos

The coach, thick and bald, marched from his office and blew his whistle. "Toes on the black line, gentlemen."

After a moment of hesitation, the ninth graders fell into formation. His bellowing voice echoed through the gym as he called off their names. After each one, he looked up and nodded.

"Peretti, William." Coach V glanced up and paused.

William's eyes locked onto the glass enclosure that held a state trophy. The only trophy ever won by the school. The bronze award now looked dusty and discolored. The coach waited for an acknowledgment and seemed to be studying the boys who were wearing jeans or shorts, hoodies or T-shirts, sneakers or Nike slides.

"Here," William said from the back. He focused on the clock behind the coach and jammed his hands into his pockets.

"Are you Billy's kid?" the coach asked.

William gave only a slight nod. Usually, his hand shot up like a rocket, and he would answer in a firm and deliberate voice. But not today, not with this man. Instead, he studied the coach. Everyone called him Coach V. He wore a white, long-sleeve T-shirt that bulged at the arms and chest. His black warm-up pants made him look threatening, while the red whistle around his neck seemed to give him that *I'm-in-charge* look.

"I played ball with your dad." Coach V tossed him a half-smile that dissipated as he called the next name.

William shrugged and remembered how strange the man had looked at the funeral. He was wearing a suit and just kept staring at his father, Billy, who was lying inside the casket.

"Don't worry," Danny whispered. "No one cares."

William did listen to the whispers and tried to ignore the fingers that were pointing in his direction. Instead, he turned his attention back to the clock and watched the second hand slowly tick, as if gravity were somehow holding it back.

The coach handed a stack of papers to a tall boy wearing a Lakers T-shirt. "Travis, take one and pass the rest down." Coach V walked in front of the boys like a sergeant inspecting his recruits. "Basketball tryouts Monday. If you're interested, have your parents sign the consent form." He stopped in front of William. "I'll hold a spot for you."

"Ah … sure." William stared at the floor as he answered.

Coach V turned and addressed the class. "Change and be back in five."

As the boys ran to a door at the far end of the gym, William paused. He hated locker rooms. The pungent odor of testosterone and chlorine always burned his nose. He snaked through the gray metal jungle to an isolated corner and stripped. He hung his pants next to his shirt. Opening his backpack, he pulled out the new clothes and stared at the price tags. They were a last-minute purchase. William tugged at the plastic loop.

Travis walked up and bumped William's shoulder hard enough for his head to bang into the locker door. "So, Willy does want to play some ball?"

William looked up and frowned.

"Stop it, Travis," Danny shouted as he laced up his shoe.

Several students formed a ring around William and Danny and Travis.

His father's words echoed inside William's head. He was only seven at the time and staring out at the huge court that looked larger than a football field. *All the kids are as nervous as you are.* His father was down on one knee, their faces nose to nose. *Block it out. Drive hard to the bucket and finish like I showed you. Don't back down — ever. Guys love to jaw-jack and knock you off your game. Believe me. I know. I was one of the best.*

"Because your daddy was something special don't mean you're automatically on the team," Travis whined.

William's heart pounded as if he were in the final minutes of a tied game with no time-outs remaining. He squeezed his left hand, creating a fist.

Danny jumped up and stood in front of William. Travis towered over Danny. "No one's guaranteed anything," Danny said, "except that you're a jerk."

"My ass." Travis took a step, sandwiching Danny between him and William. "There ain't no sympathy for you cause you found your old man swinging." He pointed toward the gym. "You gotta prove it out there."

Danny placed his hands on Travis to hold him back.

"See you at tryouts … bitch." Travis reached around Danny and jammed his finger into William's chest. "That is, if you're man enough to show up." He turned and walked away.

William changed into his street clothes and told Coach V that he wasn't feeling well and would visit the nurse's office. The nurse would keep him busy, and the gym period would be over.

William trudged the three miles home. It was warm, and he had stopped to take off his sweatshirt. As he stuffed his things into his backpack, someone called out his name.

"Why didn't you wait for me?" Danny ran up, panting.

"In a hurry," William replied.

"Wanna come over? Mom said you should stay for dinner. I bought a new video game."

"I wish I could." William kept his eyes on his backpack.

The two were always together, either playing video games, throwing baskets, or fishing off Lake Michigan's jetties. William's refusal was a rare occurrence.

"It's a hard day for your family and all … but if you change your mind."

William nodded. "I won't. I mean, I can't. Not today."

William climbed the steps of the home his parents bought after his grandfather passed. Billy, his dad, wanted to be close to his mother in case she needed help. Billy planned on remodeling the house from its original orange-and-brown motif but never got around to it.

William dropped his backpack into a chair. "Mom?" He entered her bedroom and called again. "Mom?" He checked the kitchen and noticed that the door to the basement was open. He paused and his heart pounded. Placing his hands on either side of the molding, he leaned into the opening and shouted, "Mom? You down there?"

"Doing laundry," his mother yelled back. "Be up in a minute."

William took in a deep breath and sat at the kitchen table. His hands shook and his mind reeled. The breakfast dishes were still on the table, along with a grocery list he had left for his mother. He piled the plates into the sink, rinsed them, and set them in the dishwasher.

His mother entered carrying a basket of clean clothes. "Can you fold these for me? I'll start dinner."

William stared at the basket. The whites were a slight tinge of pink, and his mother's leggings looked as if they had shrunk to half their original size. His mother usually tossed half her clothes away after washing them just once. The last item he picked out was a frayed T-shirt his mother wore to bed each night. He held it up, careful not to touch the holes, and rubbed his fingers across the red Horlick Rebels logo. When his mother entered the bathroom, he pulled the shirt to his nose, praying for a hint of his father's aftershave. All that lingered was the musty scent of laundry that had sat too long in the washing machine.

After dinner, he cleared the table while his mother smoked on the back porch. He slid her untouched food into a container and set it in the refrigerator on top of three others. Every Sunday, he'd clean out the fridge, washing the glass and plastic for the next week. If his mother were hungry, she'd snack on potato chips or pretzels and cheese, washing it down with a can of soda.

"You better get on your schoolwork," his mother said through the screen door as the smoke streamed out through her nose. She stared into the night sky and added, "I'm going out."

His mom's name was Anita. Sometimes he saw her as Mom, sometimes as Anita. Tonight, Anita had decided to leave him home alone.

After smashing out the cigarette on the railing, she walked into the kitchen. Gone was her curvy figure from a few years ago, replaced with jeans that hung low on her hips and boney shoulders that protruded out from her tank top. Her dyed, blonde hair with the black roots seemed to match the dark circles under her eyes. Something she could no longer conceal with just makeup.

William studied her. "Why?"

"I need a break." Anita made a circular motion with her hand. "From all of … this." She patted his shoulder. "Don't wait up."

"I understand." But he didn't understand. He placed his backpack on the table and unzipped the flap.

Anita grabbed her purse and walked out the front door with a cigarette hanging from her lips.

"Today of all days … really, Anita?" He said it out loud once the door had slammed shut and she could no longer hear. William spread out his homework on the dining room table. He pulled out his biology book and pulled out the letter from Coach V again reading over the words.

Why does everyone assume I'm like my dad?

They had the same name, same eyes, and same hair coloring. But that was where the similarities ended. William studied in the library and had entered high school with straight A's. He blended in with the crowd at lunchtime and focused on only one sport. The one everyone expected him to play.

His father, on the other hand, had lived in the gym, a three-sport athlete who constantly practiced, trying to hone his skills. On the weekends, Billy left his textbooks in his locker and drove around town looking for any party that he could find.

William's stomach tightened as he stuffed the paper into a book, confident in his decision not to accept Coach V's offer. He worked for a couple of hours, finishing his biology, math, and English assignments, thinking he would stay up until Anita returned.

Mom wouldn't need help getting undressed and into bed, but Anita would. Even so, he fell asleep with his head resting on his outstretched arm. At two in the morning, the front door opened. He was startled as Anita entered with a stranger. The guy was tall and thin and wore work boots. His pants were soiled, and he was wearing a silver, buttoned-plaid, western-style shirt. Engrossed in conversation, they didn't realize William was in the room. The guy leaned over and said something to Anita, and she gave a fluttery laugh. She leaned up to kiss him and William stood.

"Anita?" William stated.

"Why are you still up?" Anita's words were slurred. She slung her arm around the man's shoulder. "It's a school night."

The man tipped the brim of his baseball cap back and threw out a quizzical look. He swayed as if it were difficult to stay upright. "You didn't tell me you had baggage."

William collected his schoolwork as Anita shooed him with her hands. The man grabbed his mother's ass, and she wildly slapped at his arm.

"This was a mistake," she said. "You need to leave."

The man glanced over at William and frowned. "Remember, lady. You picked me up."

His mother forced the man out the door and locked it.

William crawled into bed, listening to his mother crying. He placed his hands behind his head and stared up at the illuminated plastic stars he had arranged to look like the Milky Way galaxy. It was a project his father helped him finish while he was in the fifth grade. As a kid, Billy wanted to be an astronaut. He had memorized the position of the planets in the night sky. While on Boy Scout campouts, or having a beer in the backyard, or roasting marshmallows at a neighborhood get-together, Billy often pointed up at a red dot and explained how he'd love to take a year-long journey to the alien world. William remembered Billy sitting on his bed with the instructions and pointing out where the stickers should go. William had stood on a ladder and penciled out each one. Now, as with most things in this house, it seemed to represent something that didn't exist anymore.

The back screen door slapped shut, and William imagined Anita with smeared mascara, lighting one cigarette after the other, trying to calm herself down. In the morning, she'd be curled up in a blanket, sleeping in the recliner until he woke her for breakfast. His mother would then wander into the kitchen with an afghan around her shoulders, and William would place a cup of coffee in front of her. He would not bring up the night's events because the same questions would always come up. "How could your father leave us? Didn't he love us anymore? Were we not enough for him?"

William cut his grandmother's grass every Sunday after she returned from church. He took over the chore from his father and never asked for money, even though his grandmother, Nonna, would shove twenty dollars into his pocket. He used every excuse he could think of – the yard is small – it only takes fifteen minutes to mow – it's a labor of love – Dad would want me to. But she never budged. She'd hug him and say, "Let me treat you. Go to a movie or get a burger. Do something fun for yourself."

He woke early and tiptoed through the house. Anita had left the back door open, and he gently pushed on the screen door, holding it so it wouldn't bang shut. Anita rolled over on the sofa but did not wake. He headed for the small coffee shop that was two blocks away for a muffin and hot chocolate.

Near the corner, he paused. Danny's mother was kneeling on an old towel, cutting wilted flowers with a hooked knife. Five potted mums sat next to her, waiting to be planted. They exchanged waves.

"Are you coming over tonight?" she asked. "I'm making your favorite … Costco's chicken pot pie."

"I'll check with my mom," he said with a smile.

It was a short three-block walk to Nonna's house from the coffee shop. He would use the mower bag to catch the grass clippings and the maple leaves that were now the color of fireballs. He punched in the garage code and waited as the motor squealed. His grandfather's old mower sat next to the tool bench. Nonna tried to convince William to take the saws, screwdrivers, pipe wrenches, and hammers home, but the shrine was too comforting to visit.

He pushed the mower and carried the red gas container outside. The cap was tight, so he wrenched it open with both hands. The tank was empty. With the coach's letter heavy on his mind, a slight wind pushed his thoughts into motion. The old basketball hoop swayed, and the net looked rotted and weathered and was attached by only one strand. How many hours had he and his dad practiced here? His mind wandered to summer holidays – barbecues in this backyard with family and friends, games with the neighbors, stories of Billy making the winning shot at the state championship game, beer-drinking, backslapping conversations where everyone wanted to be his father, and the expectations that William would follow in his father's footsteps.

"Won't the mower start?" Nonna asked, rubbing her arthritic hands together.

Her gray hair was always pulled into a tight bun. He smiled as her gnarled fingers had trouble picking up silverware, let alone a tiny bobby pin. Yet she always looked neat. He expected nothing less from this Italian immigrant who worked her whole life in a book printing factory on the southside of town.

William turned and hugged her. "Nonna, I haven't tried it yet."

"Come inside, honey. I have lunch ready."

She led him into the kitchen of the two-story bungalow, where he smelled the vanilla vigil candle burning in front of a picture of the Virgin Mary. The fragrance now mixing with the cheese and noodles she'd been cooking. The house was old but spotless. The furniture was covered with blankets she'd personally crocheted, neatly stacked magazines, and a doily covering the end table where her perpetual cup of coffee sat waiting for the next episode of The Price is Right.

"Grab the plates, forks, and knives," she said as she carried a casserole to the dining room table.

At fifteen, he knew he'd never tell her that the meal she made for him as a child was not his favorite anymore.

"I was thinking about you and your mother the other day," Nonna said.

He handed her his dish, and she heaped the yellow elbow pasta into the center.

"I should have called," William said.

"I had hoped we'd all be together." She handed him his plate back. "How is your mother?"

He shrugged. "Tough day."

She pursed her lips and gave a slight shake of her head. "I can't believe it's been two years." Nonna looked at him and sighed. "And what about you?"

"I still can't go into the basement."

"I don't know why your mother wanted to stay in that house, knowing that Billy ..." Her voice cracked and she focused on the napkin that draped across her lap. "She's going to have to find a job sooner or later. How long can the insurance money last?"

William picked up his fork and knife and stared at his food.

"I'm sorry, I have no right." Nonna fumbled with her napkin. "It's her life." She stood and returned with a small bowl. "I almost forgot. I went to the orchard this week." She spooned two helpings of apple sauce onto his plate.

A car stopped across the street and honked. Two young boys jumped into the back seat with their gloves and bats. The bay window was now framed with evergreen branches.

"I think we need to trim the bushes," William said. "Didn't Nonno trim them in the fall?"

"I think so," she replied. "Remember the time you and Nonno were using the electric hedge clipper, and he cut the power cord." She laughed. "Sparks flew everywhere. I thought you were going to be electrocuted."

"Dad pulled me away."

"Nonno was so upset. If something had happened to you, he couldn't have lived with himself."

William looked around and studied the pictures of his father that were arranged on the china cabinet. The walnut furniture still held a shrine to Nonna's only child – photos from grade school, sport teams up through high school, and his one year playing in college. It seemed odd that she kept them all these years.

Dad would have been forty in February. "When did Dad get so good?"

"Oh, I don't know. If Nonno were here, he'd be able to answer that question. I was jaded." She gave him a pained smile. "He was always the best player in my mind."

William pushed his food around on his plate. "Do you remember a guy Dad played with by the name of Vukovich?"

"Darrell? I haven't heard that name in a long time." She wiped her mouth. "He grew up just around the block."

"Did they get along?"

"Your dad and Darrell?" She straightened as if the question had somehow pierced her chest. "Didn't have a mean bone in his body. Some people didn't like him, but I don't think Billy was one of 'em."

"He's my gym teacher, and he wants me to try out for basketball."

Her body shifted ever so slightly in the chair. "What do you want?"

"I never want to play again."

Lines drew across her forehead. "You don't have to do anything you don't want to."

William placed his fork on the table. "Can I ask you something?"

"Of course, honey. Anything."

"I don't get it." William looked away as he searched for words. "Why die with your high school jersey on?"

She reached across the table and cupped his hand. The gentle squeeze from her crooked fingers felt somewhat odd.

"God only knows why people do what they do," she whispered. "It was a happy time in his life. Maybe he wanted to remember that feeling."

William pulled his hand away and crossed his arms. "He only cared about sports. Nothing else."

"He was sick, Willy, in a lot of pain. I'm not sure sports had anything to do with it."

It had everything to do with it. After his father blew out his knee, there were no more games to play. The notoriety and clapping had stopped. When William found him in the basement, his body was not that of an athlete who could rip off a hundred sit-ups in under five minutes, but an overweight Amazon fulfillment worker who had trouble sleeping longer than an hour or two a night. William squeezed his eyes shut and removed his glasses.

"Your dad was a nervous kid who couldn't sit still. Nonno got him into basketball to try and channel his energy." She pulled her chair closer to the table and stared at William. "Don't blame him. It's my fault. Your mother tried, but when the anxiety was too much … he never wanted to leave …" She covered her mouth with both hands.

"I hate him!" William admitted his feelings for the first time. "And I hate basketball!"

"*William* … he's still your father. Remember that. And all the good things he ever did for you."

William prepared dinner for his mother and left it on the stove. Since the anniversary of his father's death, she'd been on her best behavior and actually attempted to clean the house. It was a meager task of vacuuming and running a cloth over the furniture. At least it was something. They hadn't spoken since the stranger incident, and if his mother followed her usual patterns, she'd come home with her hair fixed and her nails freshly painted. Her endless shopping sprees, buying him nothing he needed, were to make up for the times she had fallen off the wagon. And the alcoholic world that was only Anita's would start up all over again. He waited for her to sit outside to smoke and then scribbled her a note that he would be at Danny's and be home by ten. He left out the front door without saying goodbye.

After dinner, Danny and William stood in front of the 65-inch monitor with two lounge chairs sitting idle behind them. A large bowl of popcorn was on the end table in the middle of the room. The surround-sound speakers blared as the new video game barked out commands from the avatar characters that marched across the screen. The friends played for about an hour without conversation other than an errant comment. *Nice kill. You're in my territory. I won a victory umbrella.*

William laughed when Danny's avatar was hung up in a canyon and couldn't find its way out.

"What are you doing tomorrow?" Danny asked.

"It's Monday. We've got school."

"I meant after?"

"Why? Wanna go fishing? I hear the coho are running."

"No," Danny said, thumbing a controller. "We're going to tryouts."

William smashed a button to disable his virtual opponent. He eyed the popcorn.

Danny sat in a chair and turned to William. "If Travis wasn't such a dick, would you go?"

"It's not about him." William shook his head.

"You know it's not his fault. Travis' dad's a blowhard, and he never shuts up." Danny paused. "My mom said it's not fair what happened to you. It's clouding your judgment. She thinks your dad would want you to play."

"Well, then your mom's a dick." William hit a button and a new game started. "Look, I'm sorry. I shouldn't have said ..." He took in a deep breath.

"Everyone knows you're the best point guard at school. Everyone, including Coach V. You always have been," Danny whispered. "Since first grade."

William dropped the controller and stood. Before stepping out the door, he looked over at his friend and shrugged.

Entering through the backdoor, he found a note to wake up his mother. It seemed that she needed to talk to him. Instead, William went straight to bed.

William woke at six and entered the kitchen. It was still dark, and the only light was the one over the sink. It cast an orange silhouette around his mother who was sitting at the table with a cup of coffee. He turned on the overhead light.

"You're up early." William pulled out the cereal and shook the box. He grabbed two bowls.

"I'm not hungry." She took a sip and glared at him. "Why didn't you wake me last night?"

"Your room was dark."

Anita pulled a cigarette out of the pack. She wielded it between her fingers like a weapon. "Your grandmother called last night. She's worried about you." Her posture straightened. Her tone more confrontational.

He pulled out a gallon of milk. "At least somebody is."

"I may not be the best parent right now …" Anita's face scrunched as she lit the cigarette and took in a deep draw. "But have some god-damn respect for your father. He was a good man for Christ's sake."

"He's not here anymore, is he?" William opened the drawer and pulled out a spoon. "You are. And I'm the one who's got to deal with that."

"Your grandmother said that you hated your dad. So don't make this about me."

"Do you ever think about what I need or how I'm feeling?"

She held up the announcement from the coach. "I'm asking now. Danny's mother said that you're not going to try-outs. Last year for you. Why not?"

He filled the bowl with cereal and milk and shoved a spoon full of Frosted Flakes into his mouth.

Anita wadded up the paper and threw it at him. As it bounced off his arm, she yelled out, "He wanted you to be better than he ever was."

He stared at her. "It's not my dream to be known as Billy's son. The man who couldn't cope with reality and who hung himself in our basement … for his son to find. I don't want anyone's pity … not even yours."

The tip of her cigarette glowed a bright red, and the cloud of smoke she exhaled surrounded her face. Anita pointed the Virginia Slim at him and said, "If you don't need either of us anymore, then wash your own fucking clothes." The smoke dissipated as Anita jammed the stub into the bowl that William had placed in front of her. "You never knew him as I did."

William was ready to leave. When things were bad at home, he'd stay at Danny's for a few days until Anita came to her senses. He made a mental note of what to take to his best friend's house. This time, maybe he wouldn't come back.

"I loved watching your father compete," his mother said in a slow, calm voice. "I never cared how good he was or if he even won the game. It was because he was so different. So confident." She cocked her head to one side as if trying to see past William. "It made everyone around him play better." She reached for another cigarette then pulled back her hand. "I wish you'd reconsider trying out for the team."

William stared at his mother. "I can't do anything for you or him anymore."

At a little after three, William walked to the gym. He stood in the middle of the open door while Travis and Danny ran two-on-two drills along with twenty other boys. The sun streaked through the windows, barred only by the metal grates. The volume in the gym echoed into the hallway. Shouts from Coach V and squeaking sneakers filled his ears.

Turning to leave, he paused.

"Hey, can you get that?" Travis yelled out.

A ball bounced William's way and landed at his feet. He picked it up and could smell the leather. Something from across the court grabbed his attention. His mother was staring down at him from the bleachers. She was wearing clean clothes and had fixed her hair into a ponytail. Something he hadn't seen for a while. He imagined her twenty years earlier sitting in the same spot and perhaps watching Billy. William rolled the ball around in his hand as Coach V and the other players watched.

"We need you!" Travis shouted. "Come on."

William pinned the ball under his arm, turned, and walked onto the court.

A Father's Son

Nick Tseffos

Lynn's thoughts …

Denial, anger, bargaining, depression, and acceptance – the five stages of grief and all are included in this short story about a death in a family. A young man is trying to survive the internal struggles of where to place his anger. Does he blame his mother? Does he blame a sport? Does he blame himself?

When a child loses a parent, it is difficult for them to continue within the normalities of life. They want everything to be as it was before … but nothing ever is and that sharp pain is ever present.

In this story, our main character wants to play with the rest of the team, but when the coach remembers his father, the flash of reality is too much. It is therefore easier to walk away. Working through his father's death, the boy must also survive the struggles of his daily relationships.

It's funny how a death can change so much in such a short amount of time. This author is able to add subtlety to how our regular life can be disrupted by allowing us to walk in the character's shoes. This family's clothes have changed color – white to pink. The mother no longer cooks or cleans. Then, when the mother picks up a stranger and brings him home, the main character, the boy, comes to her rescue and protects her from herself. Something we cannot do when our grief is too loud and masks the truth.

We follow the main character through the various stages of grief. And the author does a wonderful job showing us how we try to keep reality ever present in an ever-changing world. As an example, the mother is living in an alternate reality by not eating or sleeping. However, she does make a comment about the importance of his homework, which is an attempt to bring back the normality. Then, the son mows his grandmother's lawn and again … normality. In the end, the boy walks bravely back onto the court to face the challenges with dignity and respect. A great ending to an otherwise sad situation.

A Father's Son

A Very Unusual Day

Rose Heaser

OUR FAMILY OF six moved to Neosho, Missouri in 1969, trailing the purchase of Neosho Charcoal Products, Inc. We were accustomed to moving and adapting to change, but we were not expecting it to create such a very unusual day.

Dave loved working outdoors. When he worked for Humphrey Contracting, he was a great tractor operator of a D9 Caterpillar. However, the position required constant relocation. It wasn't long before Hump had him bidding and running their jobs. The company cleared land for dams and new highways from the Yellowtail Dam in Wyoming all the way to roads in New Jersey and New York. Now, he just wanted to enjoy being home at night for a home-cooked meal with his family. He realized that he had missed much of his children's younger years.

Dave had experimented with making charcoal by burning the cleared trees and then smothering the flames with dirt. It worked but proved to be expensive. When the opportunity presented itself to purchase Neosho Charcoal Products, he decided to take a chance.

Neosho Charcoal Products consisted of eight cement-block kilns the size of small houses. The kiln had six holes around the bottom to control air flow, which allowed the fire to burn hot enough to turn wood into charcoal. The plant was located on twenty acres, seven miles out in the country off Highway HH. The only building, other than the kilns, was a 4' by 4' structure shaped like an outhouse that housed the company's telephone. To manufacture charcoal, a fire box was built in the center of the kiln before filling it with wood slabs from floor to ceiling. After lighting the fire box, the steel doors were shut. With no temperature controls, Dave ran the work by the seat of his pants.

I was a petite blonde with short hair who was a stay-at-home mom except when working the books for the plant. When Kathee and Jim were in the sixth grade, we were surprised with twin girls. It changed our lives, but they were such happy babies. We soon accepted the change and enjoyed the addition to our family.

Jim, our son, played cornet and trumpet in the junior high band and was a first-class Boy Scout. His troop was planning on attending the World Boy Scout Jamboree in Japan the following summer. He was a great big brother, as he was so helpful with the twin girls.

Kathee, our daughter, was petite with long, blonde hair. Just before we moved, she was in a modeling class that was sponsored by Sears. Dave encouraged her to model as he thought they might convince her to cut her hair. The modeling class ended with a style show. The announcer introduced our daughter with, "Kathee's blue eyes and stylish blonde coiffure compliment her outfit of …"

I looked at Dave and said, "You lost that one!"

When we moved to Neosho, we rented a house but agreed to allow the realtor to show the place to potential buyers. Since our money was spent on the purchase of the business, which needed a new tractor and an 18-wheeler dump truck to haul bulk charcoal to the Jay Hawk Briquetting plant in Chetopa, Kansas, we were forced to rent.

The house had a tall living room with windows that overlooked a large, grassy backyard. The oblong, pecan-colored, paneled kitchen was complimented by a white, oval table with turquoise chairs. Two highchairs were on one end of the room and the refrigerator, stove, and sink on the other. With lots of cupboards and counter space, I was quite happy.

There were only three bedrooms, so the girls shared the master that had two closets. Kathee was not a happy teenager with eighteen-month-old sisters, Marla and Carla, examining and handling her things all the time. Therefore, she kept their clothes in the smaller closet and claimed the top drawers where the girls couldn't reach. The two cribs were on the far side of the room, and Kathee grabbed the larger closet for herself. She placed a cot inside, turning the closet into her bedroom. She hung a shoe rack with pockets to hold her personal items. It left no room to move around, but she could shut her door and keep out the little ones.

Things were great for the first several months.

The school year started, and one evening, Jim had a Boy Scout meeting for the families going to Japan. The day was full for everyone. Jim and Kathee attended band practice in the morning and marching practice after school, which meant a trip in the morning and afternoon with the two little ones.

When I picked her up after practice, Kathee wasn't happy. Her band director had assigned her the bass drum for marching. Kathee was about four feet in height and not quite eighty pounds.

"I want to quit band," she stated. "Mr. Banks doesn't like me. He made me carry that big drum everywhere. I can't even see over the thing. I can hardly carry it ... it's so heavy. And ... all the other drummers are boys. Not *one* girl plays the drums."

"Let's talk about it another time when you're not so tired," I replied. "You used to like playing the drums." I started supper. "You had a long day, and it was your first day of marching. You're just exhausted and not happy. In fact, we've all had a long day."

Earlier, I had run errands, which was a large task with two little ones. It was hard getting anything accomplished while holding their hands. We had a huge side-by-side stroller that turned into a buggy. But it was heavy to load and unload at every stop, and most places did not have aisles wide enough. The precious time the twins were good while shopping was overruled with a most annoying question. "Are they twins?" I would simply nod and hold back my smart-alecky remarks.

Supper was slipped in somehow with everyone stacking their dirty dishes in the sink, since our dishwashers were all attending the scout meeting. Marla and Carla were busy seeing how many toys they could pull out and soon had the living room littered with toys.

The scout meeting was the first planning meeting for the families of the boys going to Japan, and it lasted way past our bedtime. Dave was an early riser, which meant that we turned in once we returned home.

When the kilns were burning, Dave always checked the fires before daylight and would return for breakfast. He headed out the next morning as usual, and it wasn't long before the phone rang. It was Dave.

"A kiln exploded! Can you bring me the camera? I need it documented. The company carries insurance, and I'll have to file a claim."

"I'll be there as soon as possible."

I woke Jim to let him know where I was going. I didn't want to wake the little ones this early as it was still dark outside. I left a note asking Jim and Kathee to feed the girls and themselves some cereal, and I would return as soon as possible.

I took our Polaroid that Dave received for Christmas and stopped by Wolf's Quick Trip to grab a throw-away camera. After I dropped them off, I ran back to town for tarps. By the time I returned home and walked in the door, the house had become a disaster area. Breakfast food and dishes covered the kitchen table and counters with drawers left partway open. The living room floor was covered with toys. No beds were made and clothes, both clean and dirty, decorated the floors. The bathroom was unexplainable.

Kathee and Jim had missed the bus and needed a ride to school. I dressed the girls as quickly as possible and drove with the little ones screaming, "Dog, dog, dog," whenever they saw someone walking their dog along the way.

"Good, there're no lines to wait in," I said as I pulled up to the school.

Kathee spoke first. "There's no one here. I told Ralph that I would meet her on the bench in the entrance hall. She's probably wondering why I'm not here yet."

"The bell rang already," Jim said. "Can't we stay home? Can't we just take a note tomorrow?"

"No, you cannot," I replied. "Have a wonderful day, and I'll see you this afternoon."

I retraced my route home with the girls again screaming, "Dog! Dog! Dog!"

The phone was ringing as I walked in. It was Maxine, the realtor. "I would like to show the house this morning. The people are from out of state and will not be here beyond today."

"It's been a very unusual morning, and I can't handle it today."

Maxine sighed. "You agreed to allow entry to potential buyers."

"You also said we'd have plenty of lead time."

Maxine sighed again. "They've driven by and the house is just what they're looking for."

"We had a meeting last night, and I didn't get to tidy up before bed. This morning a kiln blew, and it just isn't possible to show the house." The phone had a thirty-foot cord that allowed me to talk and clean anywhere in the kitchen. After haggling for a few more minutes, I gave in. "Give me a couple of hours. I'll do what I can."

I'd been working with the twins to use the potty with not much success. To keep the girls occupied and not create an even bigger mess, I brought out the two potty-chairs, sat them in front of the TV, and turned-on Sesame Street.

"Sit down and see what story Big Bird has for you today," I said.

I started cleaning by stuffing the random toys into the hall closet that at least cleared a path to the front door. I shoved in the last of the push toys and slammed the door shut. I heard a thump in the closet but had no time to investigate as the doorbell rang.

When Dave had left that morning, he planned to return for breakfast. He had slipped on his dress shoes, which meant that his dusty, charcoal-covered work boots were still blocking the front door. I had left through the garage and didn't see them, or I would have taken them to him. As I bent down to move the boots, I heard a horrible sound. A *rip* ... my pants had just split open.

And ... *there* was Maxine and her buyers!

This can't be happening ...

I couldn't turn my back to them with no butt in my britches. Therefore, I had to keep them corralled.

"Good morning," I said through a false smile. "Please, come in."

The hallway was the only clean spot in the house. At the end of the hallway was the closet where I had stashed the toys.

Maxine walked in and started with her realtor spiel. "This house has so much storage space," she said as she opened the door to the hall closet.

The toys that had been stuffed inside now tumbled into the hallway.

"Oh my," Maxine said.

As she headed toward the living room, everyone received the full view of the disastrous kitchen. It was becoming harder by the moment to keep a pleasant smile on my face. Maxine pushed aside the toys with her foot to make a path while directing the buyers to the living room where the little girls were sitting on their potties.

"The living room has such a lovely view of the large backyard –"

The little girls were so excited that they stood and yelled out, "Poo poo!" They had made fragrant remains inside their potties and both were happily jumping around with unwiped, dirty bottoms.

With my hands on my hip, I glared at Maxine as the resentment in my heart sank. I just shook my head and shrugged.

Needless to say, the buyers did not buy the house, and Maxine never pulled that one on me again. It was such a very unusual day.

Lynn's thoughts …

Oh … the struggles of a family move.

Something that *everyone* hates, but also something that *everyone* must do … at least from time to time. Then let's consider the raising of young children that can present a challenge in and of itself. But when you add in an age gap, the challenges widen along with the birthdays.

I recently experienced a move from a large house to a much smaller one. The children adapted, although they struggled with where to put their treasures. There just wasn't enough room.

Our author's example of how the eldest daughter picked a closet for her bedroom definitely captured how our children are able to adapt and overcome. For some reason, it is much easier for them than for us oldies. The last *word* of the title, however, should probably be switched to life. Why? Because *every* day in a mother's world is unusual. No two days are ever the same.

The day started off bad enough when the husband's company had an explosion. But to add to it the distraction of the little ones in potty-training mode, an insistent realtor, frustrated teens, a messy house, and ripped britches, well … let's just say that anyone with children has been there and done that.

The two little girls definitely summed it up by proudly declaring that it was all "poo-poo." I cannot say how many times I have stated that the whole world had gone to poo!

A Very Unusual Day

 ABSOLUTION AT THE DINER

Tia Foisy

Russell shifted atop the plush diner seat and pushed a roughened hand across the tweed of his best Sunday pants. A grunt came with the motion – aged body protesting before it was given permission to do so. There was an aching in his knees that hadn't let up in days.

The weatherman still isn't calling for rain.

Catherine sipped from a cooled cup of tea, pulling the liquid onto her tongue with a noise that could only be called obnoxious. In here however, her slurping couldn't be heard over the clatter of kitchen pans or the buzzing lights above their heads. And, in here, she couldn't care less.

Between them sat a half-eaten piece of dry chocolate cake. A smear of icing crossed the ceramic tabletop, decorating a trail of crumbs toward Russell's mouth. The small, circular plate was placed closer to her.

His arms were longer, after all.

It would be their youngest son's twenty-third birthday, if he hadn't been laid to rest in a too-small casket a decade prior. Every year since, they sat in these very seats, engulfed by the silence that befell their marriage that one fateful night.

Absolution at the Diner

Losing Sammy had placed a divide between them. Drew a line right down the center of their family. Russ on one side with a fistful of whiskey, and Catherine with her sober eyes on the other. Their remaining children played a balancing act of tiptoeing on top. He blamed himself more than he blamed the weather or the deer in his headlights or the black ice. He blamed himself because he was the one to live daily with the memory of holding their dying boy in his arms, knowing it was the end. The tears that hadn't frozen to his face on that blistering night fell to mix with Samuel's blood.

Barely conscious and body convulsing, the boy had to listen to his father's blubbering about how he wanted to avoid hitting the deer.

"I didn't see any animal," Sammy had whispered.

Those last few words stuck with Russell, remained with him like a concrete knot churning inside his chest that demanded his attention at the least opportune times. Some days, it felt like a heart attack lying in wait. Other days, an attack that he prayed for.

He never hit the animal. Supposed it had pranced off and disappeared into the tree line, but Sammy never saw it, and Russ never stopped thinking about how tired he'd been on that drive home. How many hours he'd worked and how many glasses he'd drank.

"Cake's always dry," he said. "Ain't half as good as yours."

They'd desperately tried to survive their private drought. Just the two of them, bound to one another by a promise that was made when they were only children themselves, having been dying to make it out alive.

"Doesn't matter," she replied. Her attention refused to leave the table.

She was right. It'd been Sammy's favorite, either way.

Catherine focused on the way her napkin absorbed the liquid from her discarded teabag. She'd always been harder and colder than her soft-hearted counterpart. She'd always wondered whether it would've been better had she gone to pick up Samuel from hockey practice that night.

Russell couldn't peel his eyes from her face. He'd made a second career out of trying to read her, out of swallowing the questions that all too often clawed their way up the back of his throat. The claws that left scratches and lacerations on their way back down. Scars for every time he didn't pry to know what was going on inside her mind.

Above the plate, their forks moved toward the final bite at the same time. A shared lack of attention tangled the prongs, creating a tiny but temporary mess of utensils until they pulled back.

"Sorry," Russell said with half the word catching in the back of his throat before he could clear it.

"It wasn't your fault," she whispered, and it was the first time she had ever said it. The first time in a decade that she looked him directly in the eyes and admitted that there'd been no crime done at the hands of her husband.

Russell's gaze turned to glass, and an imminent threat of tears welled along his bottom lashes.

The sky opened, and from their diner window, they watched together as a summer rain trickled down and dampened the soil of their small town.

- 36 -

Lynn's thoughts …

To forgive … to allow another a release from the burden of a sin … how many people can actually do this? Although, it is something that we all must do at some point during our life. But can we ever successfully walk away?

This short story brings a harsh reality to light. How long can someone carry a burden of guilt, and at what point do we simply accept the truth? At times, the pain of regret may be too much for us to understand and move on with our lives.

What I liked about this story is how the wife focuses on the way her napkin absorbs the liquid from her discarded teabag. It is at this point that the author has demonstrated how our emotions are ever fluid and ever changing. The wife had just forgiven her husband for what they always believed was his sin – the accidental death of their son.

The wife felt guilty because she didn't pick the boy up. The father felt guilty because he had several drinks. And then there is the question as to whether or not there actually was a deer in the road.

We can visualize this couple sitting alone at a table, avoiding each other's gaze … avoiding each other's admonishment. The author clearly demonstrates how they are punishing each other as they annually mourn their child's loss. Although together, they suffered alone. The two are aging now, and their pain has already destroyed their marriage. Through this story, I see a couple, separated, who meet up on an annual basis to remember. Their family divided, their world shattered. Although sad and moving, this story brings to light a harsh reality of being human … *guilt.*

Absolution at the Diner

Band of Gold

Steven Sousa

A loud and deliberate knock echoed out from the front door. Martha checked her robe before leaving her spot at the kitchen table. Two uniformed men stood looking solemn on the front porch. Martha, with her long, wavy hair and beautiful smile, nodded at them.

"Mrs. Ryne Vandermere?" the taller officer asked.

"Yes."

"I'm Officer Johansen and this is Officer Wagner," the second officer added. "May we enter?"

"Of course." Martha stood back and frowned.

After removing their hats, they entered. Wagner sat as if it were his only job. Johansen remained standing.

"What's this all about? Ryne's been away. Maybe three weeks now. Security detail … an armory or warehouse or something. He never talks much about his work. I spoke to him yesterday." Martha sat and smiled.

"No easy way to have this discussion, Mrs. Vandermere," Johansen said.

The dog barked from the next room.

"Jack!" Martha yelled out and the dog quieted.

"Your husband was manning a military warehouse just outside of Philly. There was a fire," Johansen said, lowering his eyes.

Wagner remained silent but nodded.

"He didn't make it," Martha stated.

"No," Johansen replied. "He didn't. I'm sorry. We offer our sincere condolences. He was a good man and a great soldier."

Martha raised her hand and lowered her head. As her tears fell, she held her other hand to her face.

"There is one more small matter," Officer Johansen said.

Martha nodded.

"We're here to deliver his belongings."

Martha stared at the men.

Wagner shifted in his seat, looking uncomfortable.

Johansen reached into his pocket and pulled out a small cloth bag. "The fire was intense. We only found this among the debris. We assume that it's his wedding band. He was the only man on site, and if you can identify the ring, we can close this matter." Johansen handed Martha the small cloth bag. She opened it and looked inside.

"This is all that's left?"

Both men nodded. Wagner headed for the door. Johansen extended his hand but Martha ignored it. Johansen stopped at the front door and sighed. "He will be missed." And both men left.

Martha imagined that Ryne would walk through the door that afternoon just as scheduled. Maybe this was all just a bad dream, an errant thought, a worst fear being visualized inside her imagination. She stared at the ring and placed it on the table. Maybe if she didn't look at it, then Johansen and Wagner could be brushed away instead of accepted as men with grave news. Just a nightmare caused by undigested food. Perhaps she would wake up from her afternoon nap and Ryne would be standing there with a smile, waiting for a hug. They could live happily ever after just as they had planned. She could tell Ryne about her vivid dream and they could laugh about it. Then he would assure her that he'd never leave her to become a widow.

Martha snapped out of her trance and walked into the next room. Maybe she was right and it was all just a dream. She stopped and glanced back at the table. The ring was gone. Jack panted and the ring fell from his mouth with a clank on the hard floor, shattering her delusion.

"Jack, no!" Martha scolded.

The dog licked up the ring and it disappeared.

Martha pried open his mouth and searched through the dripping goo. The ring was gone. All that was left of her marriage now rested deep inside her dog. She laughed and cried, feeling both absurd and sad. The happenings of the morning had already felt surreal. Now she wondered if she had lost her mind. Martha loaded Jack into the car and headed for the vet.

"It will pass," the vet said with a chuckle.

"Pass?"

"Yes. Within the week, it'll traverse through the dog's digestive system and pass right through."

"A week?" Martha repeated. "Will it hurt him?"

"No, not at all. Jack'll be fine." The vet smiled, reminding her of a used car salesmen. "It will pass."

"I need that ring!"

"Over the next few days, check his stool. You'll find it."

"What if I don't?"

"You will."

"Within the week?" she asked.

"Yes. It will pass. If it doesn't pass in a week, you'll have a dead dog."

"What do I do then? I need that ring."

"It will pass."

"But if the dog dies, what then?" Martha felt her mind moving into panic mode.

"If it becomes necessary, the ring can be surgically removed from the dog."

"So if I don't find it ... I come back and you'll surgically remove the ring?"

"We don't do that here. Not on deceased animals."

"Can you remove it from a living one?"

"Martha. It will pass. Jack will be fine. Inspect his stool. You'll find the ring."

Martha huffed and smiled and grabbed onto the leash. On the way to the car, Jack veered toward a small patch of grass and squatted. Martha sighed as she marched the dog back into the office.

"Excuse me," she whispered to the receptionist. "Do you have a pair of medical gloves I could have? I must check his …"

The receptionist smiled and nodded. "One second."

Martha returned outside and knelt down. She pressed on the dog's … with the tip of her gloved index finger. When the … stuff … was flat, she sighed – no ring. She was relieved it was over but dreaded having to check the next one. She loaded Jack into the car and drove home.

Every day she searched through Jack's … stuff … searching for the lost ring. And every day, she came up short. By the time the week was nearing its end, she stopped using gloves, no longer caring. It felt somewhat natural to her now. No ring and Martha worried that she might have missed it.

That night as she slept, she woke to the sound of Ryne walking through the front door. She grabbed him and he hugged her as if he had never left. Standing back, she opened her eyes. Her living room was empty. It was all a dream … a waking nightmare. A reminder of what could never be. Entering the kitchen, she tripped over Jack. Bending down, the dog felt cold and stiff. Martha sat on the floor next to her dog and cried.

As the morning light lit the kitchen, Martha carried her dog to her car. She showered and dressed and drove to the vet's office. She walked inside carrying Jack in her arms.

"He … he's with another client," the receptionist said. Looking at the limp dog, she held her hand over her nose and frowned. "Just a moment." She darted through the doors to the back room. After a few minutes, she returned. "Follow me. He'll see you now."

Martha walked into the room and placed Jack onto the table.

The doctor tilted his head to one side.

"It didn't pass," Martha said.

"I'm sorry for your loss," he replied.

"I need that ring and it didn't pass."

"We can't cut open a dead dog on the off chance something might be in there. You will have to let it go."

"He was alive when I brought him in last week, and now, I need that ring cut out of him. I will let it go when I have that ring in my hand."

"I can't. And even if I could, I won't. Just isn't right." The vet placed his hand to his face. "Bury your dog or put him on ice."

"Not until I get my wedding ring back."

"I'm sure your husband will buy you a new one."

Martha's tears fell. "He can't … he's dead."

The vet sighed, long and heavy. "Hold on." The vet walked into the next room and returned with a pen and writing pad. "This guy may be able to help. He lives three hours north, and you'll have to take Jack to him, but he handles things like this."

"Thank you."

The vet handed her the paper. "Buy some ice."

The air conditioning was cranked as high as it would go, and her windows were rolled down. The passenger seat was filled with bags of slowly melting ice, and Jack was perched, lopsided, on top.

"You know, Jack, you were supposed to be practice," Martha said to the dead dog. "We'll get a dog and name it Jack and see how it goes. That was what Ryne had said. I always wanted kids, but he said that they were dream-killers." Martha scoffed and continued driving. "Not if your dream is to have a family. A dog ain't no family."

Martha toggled between laughing and crying, and before long, she was wearing her shirt collar over her nose.

"I thought you stunk when you were alive!"

The ice was melting, and the passenger floor was turning into a small pond. Jack's face looked almost as if it were melting too. The features were flattened and his eyes dull.

"Why couldn't you leave well enough alone? You had to make everything difficult. Ryne only wanted a dog to keep me company while he was away. That isn't love. That's a diversion."

A strong hiss echoed out from the dog that resembled a response of agreement. Martha laughed until she hacked and gagged.

"Exactly. Now you're starting to get it. Who does he think he is? Leaving for weeks at a time and expecting me to mourn his death. Absurd! You have my back, don't you, boy? You're on my side?" Martha imagined that Jack agreed with her. "I knew I could count on you. Ryne was unreliable, couldn't even make it home on time, but you were always there."

Martha felt lost. She had begun her three-hour drive by recalibrating her sense of direction. As the outside world flew past, her inside world seemed to grow dim, as if fading into nothingness.

"Where did I go wrong, Jack?"

Jack didn't answer.

"Was it when we turned south on fifty-five? Or was it at the last intersection?"

Jack responded the way dead dogs respond by remaining silent.

"You're right, Jackie. We should stop at a motel for the night and get directions in the morning."

Martha carried the dog into the motel room and placed him in the bathtub. She was exhausted by the time the bathtub was full of ice. The stench had somewhat subsided, and she decided it was safe to keep the bathroom door open.

"In the morning, Jackie, we'll find Mr. Sewall's farm and get that ring out of you," Martha said as she lay down on the bed. "Good night, Jackie-boy." And she smiled.

That night, she had the same dream she had on most nights. She was in her own bed, and Ryne would walk through the front door. He asked if he could love her. To which she'd reply, "You can't. You're dead." Every time, she would wake standing in her living room … alone. Now, she stood in the middle of the hotel room, and it was three in the morning. She couldn't sleep. Loading Jack back in the car, she hit the road.

As the sun rose high into the sky, Martha saw it. "There it is! Sewall Farm. Jack this is it."

She pulled down a long dirt road that led to a series of barns and silos. Varying degrees of aged pickups decorated the path that led to the front door of the house. An old man opened the door before Martha could climb the stairs and knock.

"Can I help you?" he asked.

"Mr. Sewall?"

The man nodded.

"My vet gave me your name and said that you might be able to help me with my small predicament."

"And what is that?"

"I have a dog. A dead dog. And he needs surgery."

The old man shook his head and grinned. "Surgery? If he is dead, why would he need surgery?"

"He swallowed a ring. And it's important that I get it back. He swallowed it and it killed him."

"And you need the ring retrieved from inside him?"

"Yes."

"What condition do you need the ring to be in?"

"Condition? I just want that ring back," Martha replied.

"Alright, I'll get the woodchipper out."

"Woodchipper?"

"That's the easiest way to retrieve the ring. It might get a little dinged or scratched, but you'll have it by nine tomorrow morning, and I won't need to put my gloves on."

She looked back at the car and thought about Jack. She looked back at the old man and smiled. "Fine, let's do it. But … he smells."

The old man nodded. "They always do."

"This dog more than most," Martha said.

"I meant dead things …"

Band of Gold

Lynn's thoughts …

Desperation … *oh what tangled webs we weave …*

I think the woodchipper and the dead dog definitely summed up this short story about despair.

Life can really stink sometimes.

To lose all hope can push us to the brink of something we would probably most likely prefer to avoid. Martha, our center of attention in this story, stands at an edge where her world is split between an ever-growing darkness and her painful memories. Which way should she go? Martha chose the memories. And it was a ring that held those memories in place. When the dog slopped up the ring, there was no other recourse but panic.

Martha played through piles of stinky stool for days. And came up empty handed. She was desperate to have her husband back, and the only thing that remained of him was that ring. When the dog died, her memories were quickly fading along with the animal. When she placed him on ice, was that her way of putting her life on hold? Fascinating thought. And when she drove for hours searching for someone to retrieve her memories (the ring), was that her way of showing how long the path to recovery was for her?

I liked the way this author used a dog's death and desperation to demonstrate what we have to do to regain our sanity after a devastating event. What I saw in this story is how hard we must fight to recover what little hope may remain.

And even then, it can all be really stinky!

Beggars
Can't Be Choosers

Michelle Wheeler

Olivia sat in her car and used the time at the heavily, trafficked intersection to hook her phone to the radio. A man walked up and tapped on her window. He wore an expensively cut suit and carried a rather distressed-looking, vintage-style laptop bag that he had slung over his shoulder. Although he seemed in a hurry, he had an amused expression on his otherwise-handsome face.

What's he doing out here? Olivia dropped her window and smiled.

"Sorry, but I ran outta gas." He pointed to a parked car across the street. "My gauge is broken, and of all days, I left my wallet at home. Can I trouble you for a few dollars?"

Olivia never gave away money. But this guy was obviously the real deal and in need. She smiled. "Sure." Knowing that the light was about to change, she grabbed her purse and rummaged through it. She held up a twenty. "I don't have anything smaller." Although she said it aloud, she was calculating her own need.

The guy reached through the window and nodded. "Thank you. You're a lifesaver. I'll pay it forward, I promise."

"Crazy things happen." She gave him a pseudo-sympathetic smile.

"You have no idea," he replied.

The light changed and Olivia moved along with the traffic. "My good deed for the year." She felt pleased.

Olivia and her friend sat alone near the front window. Olivia raised her glass, and with a big smile, she offered a toast. "Here's to all my competitors who fortunately cannot draw a farm or anything else as good as I can." She giggled and clinked her friend's glass.

Sarah frowned. "Why do you say things like that?"

Olivia shrugged. "I was just kidding. I'm one paycheck away from eviction. Can't you just be happy for me?" She rubbed her eyes and glanced down.

"The way things come out of your mouth kinda ruins things sometimes." Sarah shook her head. "Fine ... congratulations, Olive Oil. It's a great contract and a great opportunity." She smiled and raised her glass this time. "Here's to your future." When the glasses clinked, their laughter was real.

"This route's no faster than the other one. Why can't everyone just use public transit?" As her car inched forward, Olivia gasped. She froze as she watched the same scene as yesterday play out before her. The same guy, in the same suit, and carrying the same laptop, was accepting cash from the woman in the car directly in front of her. "Whattheheck?"

The man stepped back and turned her way.

Olivia dropped her window and shouted, "Hey, asshole!"

The man turned. As recognition flickered across his face, he ran through the packed lanes and stood on the sidewalk.

The light changed.

"Oh, hell no!"

Olivia pressed her foot on the accelerator.

"He's gettin' a piece of my mind. And I'm gettin' my twenty back."

She pulled into the closest parking lot and whipped around. She sat idling at the same light, which seemed to be his territory. It was mid-morning rush hour, and Olivia felt not only rushed but fumed. She slapped the steering wheel a few times as her car inched forward. She watched as he accepted another bill from a window. Flipping on her blinker, she moved into the outer lane. Keeping her eyes locked on the man, she rolled down her window. Coasting toward him, she leaned over and yelled out.

"Ingenious idea with the suit, bro!"

He quirked a grin and extended up his middle finger. Probably wanting to avoid a scene, he darted in front of her car and aimed for the other side. She screamed out as his paled expression locked onto something behind her.

Olivia screamed as her car jerked forward, striking the man wearing the suit. A utility truck had sent them both flying until her car impacted with a utility pole. Olivia sat, dazed, with her ears ringing and her head pounding. Cars screeched to a stop and people ran into the street. A few held phones to their ears. Her car door opened with a loud crack. She stepped out on her shaky legs.

"Are you alright?" a man asked. "Maybe you should sit down." He grabbed her arm. "An ambulance is on the way."

"Is he okay?" Olivia asked.

The man shook his head. "No, he's dead."

Olivia's ears rang as she whispered, "I can't believe that I gave him my last twenty dollars."

"Jesus, lady." The man released his grip and walked away.

EMTs carted away the body as Olivia called her friend, Sarah.

The stranger stood next to a reporter whose van had been stuck in the traffic. "That's right," he said loud enough so she could hear. "The guy's lying dead in the street and that gal ..." – he pointed at Olivia – "... turns to me and says, 'I just lost my twenty dollars!' Can you believe that?"

Olivia opened the glass door and entered the conference room where her new client was waiting for her.

"Come in, Olivia." He gestured toward the table. "I'll be brief. You've lost artistic rights with TD&B. Effective immediately. There's paperwork here our attorney needs you to sign."

Olivia's eyes widened. "Why? You said my graphics were the best you've ever seen."

"This decision isn't about quality. It's about integrity." He stared at her. "What were you thinking, saying something like that on the news?"

"Like what?"

"You said, and I quote, 'I pulled back around and unintentionally killed the man.' A man you accused of extortion!"

"This is hard on me too. Not just that beggar."

He glared at her.

"That's not what I meant. What I meant to say is —"

"Stop. Let me be clear. Our partnership is terminated. All managers agree. You're toxic." He slid the papers across the table.

Olivia slipped into her tiny loft and slumped onto the edge of her unmade couch bed. Removing her heels, she listened to her voicemail.

"… it's Sarah. I can't make it tonight. I have other plans. Sorry, Olive Oil. I know you need a friend right now. I'm just not sure if it's me. Hope you un —"

Olivia tossed her phone on the blankets and sat back. She stared up at the ceiling.

Out of breath from the morning run, Olivia stood at her front door and stared at the pink sheet of paper that flapped in the wind.

FINAL EVICTION NOTICE

She ripped it off and stomped inside. The loft was filled with half-packed boxes. Most of the cupboards stood open and empty — faintly reminiscent of a paranormal film. She opened the fridge. It was empty. She grabbed her bag and headed back out.

Olivia waited in line with a sack of potatoes and a package of ramen noodles. Her phone rang and she shuffled to answer.

"Hi, Olivia. This is Randy with Baylor Insurance. Your vehicle was declared totaled by Tippin Automotive. Since you chose not to carry gap insurance, you'll be responsible for the balance of your loan. It's $12,452.67."

Olivia tapped the off button, attempting to display the normalcy of any other customer instead of one whose world was disappearing. Placing the basket on the checkout belt, her hands shook. She tried to stuff her phone into her back pocket but kept missing. A fractured giggle escaped and she muttered, "I won't have to worry about my phone much longer."

The clerk eyed her.

Olivia smiled.

The clerk tapped her foot. "$19.19."

"I have it in here somewhere." Olivia dug through her purse and glanced outside. "Oh … that's my bus." She handed the woman a twenty. She bounced on her heels and grabbed the change. She ran outside and sighed as the bus pulled away. She sat on the sidewalk below the bus sign and allowed her tears to flow. Pulling her knees close to her chest, she buried her face between her elbows. Hugging herself, she rocked. Her shopping bag stood open, and her change was scattered on the ground.

A man stopped and dropped a bill into her bag. Soon, others were passing by, and as she remained cocooned inside her pain, the sounds of cash hitting the bottom of her bag filled her ears. She glanced over her arms.

An employee from the store walked up to her. He stood tall, tapping his foot. As he crossed his arms across his chest, he said, "Ma'am, it's unlawful to solicit. Move along."

Lynn's thoughts …

Isn't the road to hell paved with good intentions? Not sure who first said it or when, but there is a lot of truth in the statement. And this short story definitely captures the flavor.

I'm not sure why our antagonist is upset … I happen to love *Coconut Found You*. But then again, that dessert is not for everyone. Is it a dessert?

I dated someone once, and I could never wish out loud around him. Otherwise, whatever I wished for he would have ready for me the following day. Some would say that his actions were a blessing. However, not necessarily … color could be off, size, shape … maybe just the excitement of doing something for myself …

Our little personal treasures that we save can never be replaced. Unfortunately, many believe that they can be and because of that attitude, they try to replace our treasures with themselves. Our author summed up the whole situation when her character said, "So much neater, babe."

So much neater for whom exactly? And what was he making neater? The cards or his life? Then again, wouldn't that be considered a form of *control?*

Our story has a just reward at the end, but then again, how many times do we actually act? Take revenge? Usually, not many. If only …

 OOKED

Michelle Wheeler

Aimee could tell what it was. Giving her boyfriend, Todd, a quick smile, she tore off the wrapping. Picking up a white plastic binder, she fought back the urge to swipe away the offensive chemical odor. The cover was blank. She thumbed through the thick, laminated pages uncertain at what she was looking at. She stopped on a page and read off the title.

"Caramel icing." In a weak voice she asked, "Are these *my* recipes?"

"Sure are. Isn't it awesome?" Todd smiled.

Aimee thought about her recipe card for caramel icing. It was written in her grandmother's own hand and on the woman's favorite, yellow-lined recipe paper decorated with delicate, printed strawberries. Grandmother had written the date, 1985, in the upper right corner when she gave it to me. Across the top and in script was, "For my little baker." The full title was, "Great Grandma Watkin's Caramel Icing." She was not Aimee's great grandmother, rather her grandmother's great grandmother. The card was over a hundred years old and smelled faintly of aged icing. The familiar smudges she recognized from when she was a child and baked with her grandmother. The card always made her smile from the precious old memories.

"How did you get my cards?" Aimee swallowed. "Are these all of 'em?"

"You bet. Last time you cooked you pulled out those dirty cards. I cleaned everything up for you. It's even tabbed. See …" He flipped over a couple of pages. "You've got Desserts, Meats, Casseroles, and so on. So much neater, babe."

Aimee nodded. She turned a page and read aloud, "Sugar cookies." She scanned the recipe. "This was Aunt Sandy's recipe for holiday pistachio nut cookies. We renamed it The Judge's Cookies when my aunt was appointed as a judge." She thought back to that family party when she had made Aunt Sandy's cookies and created a placard with the new moniker. Everyone had loved it. She'd kept the placard from the party and had paperclipped it to the recipe as a memento.

"That's the beauty of it," he said, obviously bragging. "You can just pull the paper out of the sleeve to add anything to it, but now it's protected while you have it in the kitchen. Just wipes off."

"Why didn't you just put my recipes in sleeves? Why retype 'em?"

"What? I did."

"The oven temp is missing on this one."

"Really? Hmm. Well, just Google it. I'm sure it's the same for all cookies."

Aimee sighed and smiled. "It's okay. This was *very* sweet of you. I'll just look at my actual cards and add it back on."

"What do you mean 'it's ok'?" Todd took on somewhat of a peevish demeanor. "I didn't keep 'em, babe. That's the point. You don't need 'em anymore. Look, this took me a lot of time to make. You had like a bazillion recipes. You haven't even said thank you."

"You didn't keep 'em? What are you saying?" Aimee stared at him, feeling dumbfounded.

"Christ, I did you a favor and this is the thanks I get? Here we go, it's gotta be Aimee's way or no way at all." He stood and sighed. "I thought it would give you a laugh. I gotta go to work. Why don't you make something from 'em and I'll see you tonight." He kissed her on the forehead and walked out.

Todd kicked the apartment door shut with his foot, tossing his keys on the counter.

"Aimee?"

He pulled a beer out of the fridge and walked over to the living room sofa. A box sat on the coffee table. A box he recognized from various travel stickers he had placed on it.

"Hey, why do you have my memorabilia out?"

No response.

He leaned forward and took a swig of his beer. He set the bottle on the table and pulled the box toward him. He opened it. A single white binder rested at the bottom of the otherwise-empty container. The cover was neatly typed with, "Todd's Way." He pulled it out and opened it to the first page and read.

"Disclaimer: any contents missing are purely accidental and can easily be Googled."

He turned to the next page. A white sheet simply said, "Todd's favorite, old girlfriend lying on a bed half naked." Nothing else was attached. He continued flipping through the stark white and empty pages except for the typed words. His voice rose a pitch as he read from the crisp, sterile paper that was shiny from the lamination. "Letter from Dad, summer camp, 1981. Dear son, how's my boy doing? …"

Todd threw the binder across the room. "What the fuck?"

Aimee stood in the kitchen of her new apartment next to her sister.

"Aimee," her sister said, "the family reunion is next month, and I need you to make your amazing coconut fondue."

"Of course. I can't wait."

"Me either. It's been too long since I've last tasted it."

"I meant seeing the family." Aimee laughed. "Let me just take out my trusty recipe binder," Aimee said sardonically. She opened a drawer and removed the stark, white recipe binder. The aroma of stale plastic made her nose crinkle. She flipped through the pages.

"Oh my God. You still have that thing?" Her sister gasped.

"There's no way to ever fix it. Here it is under Casseroles."

"Wait. Fondue is *not* a casserole."

Aimee rolled her eyes, stopping on the computer page that was mislabeled as *"Coconut Found You"* … She wiped at her eyes as a hysterical laugh escaped.

"Oh, you *poor* thing."

Lynn's thoughts …

Isn't the road to hell paved with good intentions? Not sure who first said it or when, but there is a lot of truth in the statement. And this short story definitely captures the flavor.

I'm not sure why our antagonist is upset … I happen to love *Coconut Found You*. But then again, that dessert is not for everyone. Is it a dessert?

I dated someone once, and I could never wish out loud around him. Otherwise, whatever I wished for he would have ready for me the following day. Some would say that his actions were a blessing. However, not necessarily … color could be off, size, shape … maybe just the excitement of doing something for myself …

Our little personal treasures that we save can never be replaced. Unfortunately, many believe that they can be and because of that attitude, they try to replace our treasures with themselves. Our author summed up the whole situation when her character said, "So much neater, babe."

So much neater for whom exactly? And what was he making neater? The cards or his life? Then again, wouldn't that be considered a form of *control?*

Our story has a just reward at the end, but then again, how many times do we actually act? Take revenge? Usually, not many. If only …

- 62 -

Do You Know

Your Neighbors?

Denise Israel

It was an embarrassing first impression, but the neighbors would just have to accept it. Her daughter was screaming as Julia pulled the pack'n'play out of the trunk. With the front door key in hand, she made her way down the short walk, the pack'n'play wedged under her arm. The key was bent from being forced too many times into the tiny hole. Another thing Adam would have to fix.

She placed the pack'n'play by the door and cringed as Emma continued to scream from the car. A can of WD-40 was sitting on the window ledge. She grabbed it and sprayed it on the lock. The oil bounced and ran down her hand. After shoving the key into the lock, she heard a click. Using her hip, she pushed. The door opened and she stumbled into the living room. The place reeked of musk, cigarettes, urine, and wet dog. Trash and the remains of fast food were strewn across the carpet.

Adam was supposed to have taken care of this. Emma cannot be in here. Would it be better on the lawn? No … ninety degrees and soon to thunder. Maybe ride around with the A/C on?

She grabbed her phone and waited as the other side rang. "Hi, this is Mrs. Edwards. I'm over at the Granger Street property. I thought you were to clean today? … How late? … Two hours?"

She picked up the pack'n'play and headed back to the car. Emma continued to scream, and her face was now a bright purple. She shoved the pack'n'play into the trunk and stood by the opened car door.

Julia lifted the crying Emma as she juggled with the diaper bag.

"It's okay. Here's some juice."

Emma quieted and grabbed the bottle. Julia placed her back into the car seat and forced a smile. She leaned against the car and pushed her shoulder-length brown hair away from her sweaty neck. After raising it up as if to make a ponytail, she let it go and sighed. She squinted at the sight of the darkening clouds.

"Hello?" a voice echoed out from across the yard. "Are you, Mrs. Edwards?"

"Yes."

"I'm Mrs. Hodges. Why are you out here in this heat?"

"Waiting on the cleaning company," Julia replied.

"You can't stay out in this heat with your child. Please, come to my house to wait."

Julia thought for only a moment before nodding. "I'd be pleased. Thank you." How nice of this lady to watch her struggle before offering help.

Fighting with the pack'n'play again, she dragged it over to the neighbor's house. After fetching Emma, Mrs. Hodges pointed to where she could set up the playpen. Emma seemed a little fussy and reached for the bric-à-brac on a nearby shelf. Mrs. Hodges smiled and handed her an unbreakable cat figurine.

Emma lay down with her thumb in her mouth and the cat in her other hand. She closed her eyes.

Julia sighed. "I'm Julia, but I guess you already know that."

"Yes." Mrs. Hodges looked to be about sixty-something with steel gray hair and light brown eyes. She was sitting ramrod straight at the edge of her wing back chair. "Let's get acquainted. I'll make iced tea."

"I'd love some."

Julia studied the décor that was devoted to cats – embroidered cat pillows, cat wall hangings, a cat umbrella stand, and on and on.

Mrs. Hodges returned and handed Julia a tall glass. "Here you are. I hope you like it. It's a family recipe."

Julia took a sip. "Wonderful. Crisp and not too sweet."

Mrs. Hodges smiled and nodded.

"You must know everything that's going on in this neighborhood."

"Well ..." – Mrs. Hodges chuckled – "... one must look out for oneself."

"Should I be afraid?"

"You can never be too cautious." Mrs. Hodges frowned. "Now that you have a child."

Julia nodded. "Emma's my whole life. I could never allow anything to happen to her."

"It's difficult to protect your child from everything. The things that befall you befall her as well."

Julia had never thought of it that way before. "Did you know the previous owners of our house?"

"Oh my, yes. We were such good friends. Our children grew up together. The Drews had two boys. We had a boy and a girl. Our children played together until they were teenagers. Then they went their separate ways."

"Why was that?"

"Their boys, shall we say, had a wild streak. The oldest was into alcohol at a very young age. Maybe I shouldn't be telling you this." She glanced over at the house with a frown.

"I'm interested in what happened."

"I guess it wouldn't hurt. The parents have long since died. May they rest in peace. The eldest, Jeremy, added rubbing alcohol to his father's gin. His father enjoyed a gin and tonic every evening."

Julia gasped. "Why would he do that?"

"Elroy had caught the boy stealing his gin and gave him a belting. That probably angered the boy enough to do what he did."

"Did Elroy die?"

"No, but he almost did. It was lucky Loretta caught him stumbling, called me, and I called an ambulance. They got to him in time."

Julia shook her head. "I'm sorry this happened to your friends."

"Things happen under our noses all the time. You just need to watch and listen."

Julia nodded.

Mrs. Hodges smiled. "Where is your husband working?"

"At university. He's an English professor."

"Ah, yes. I met him briefly when he first bought the property. You rented it out for a while, yes?"

"Yes. Was it difficult to live next to renters?"

"It was."

"I'm sorry."

Mrs. Hodges shrugged. "No sense crying over spilt milk."

Julia didn't know what to say. She sipped her tea and reached in her bag for a tissue. She wiped her forehead.

"We'll try to be better neighbors," Julia said. "I don't mean to intrude. I was waiting for the cleaning company."

Mrs. Hodges nodded. "It must be terrible in there. Those renters were the worst ever. I so wish your husband had rented to that young, red-headed woman."

Julia looked up. "What red-headed woman?"

"He didn't tell you about her?"

Julia shook her head. "If he did, I don't remember."

"Well ... *she* seemed very interested. Came twice to look at the place. They were in the house for such a long time. Stayed about forty-five minutes or so each time. I thought it curious ... that's all."

Julia shrugged. "Tell me about the tenants. What made them so terrible."

"They didn't have manners or morals. The grandparents ... I felt sorry for them. I bet they were supporting that whole group. Comings and goings all day and all night. I'd wake up at two or three in the morning to the sound of doors slamming and all sorts of cursing. Was the door hard to open? I'm sure it was because of all the slamming and such. Probably warped the frame. Cars screeching tires … hooting and a hollering. Cigarette smoke billowing from the windows. Lighters flaming in the shadows. I'd get Mel out of bed to crack a window so I could hear better.

"He said they talked of money and strange stuff about kilos and grams. Then that awful music! Cranked up so loud that if awake, one couldn't go back to sleep."

"How dreadful."

"When one is getting on in age, as we are, one becomes fearful. I'm always trying to take precautions. Your baby still sleeping? Come with me. I'll show you my garden. It won't take but a minute."

Emma looked peaceful and content. Julia hesitated but smiled and followed the woman.

"I guess it's all right," Julia whispered. "Just for a few minutes."

"Yes. Just for a few minutes."

They walked through the kitchen and stepped into the large backyard. The place had to be at least an acre. It was a world unto itself. Rosebushes of every color lined the perimeter. Julia loved the variety of colors. Each rose had a professional sign with its genus, species, and cultivar names. After a few minutes, they stepped up to a special section that Mrs. Hodges called her family plot. She said her father had once bred roses and propagated them from cuttings to create new hybrids. There was a particular flower that Mrs. Hodges pointed out.

"This is the Cynthia Roscoe Rose. As you can see, it is a black rose with a blood red interior and very sharp thorns. My father, John Roscoe, developed this hybrid in memory of my mother who was murdered in her bed when he was away on a business trip. He never got over his guilt.

"If he'd been home, maybe she would have lived, and I would have had a mother to raise me. I hope whoever killed her lived a tortured life. My father surrounded the house with this flower to make it uncomfortable for anyone to scale his fence. It was too late for my mother, but he hoped not too late for others who would hear his tale."

Julia glanced at her watch. Spellbound by the story, she didn't realize how much time had passed. "Excuse me, Mrs. Hodges. I think Emma is crying."

She darted into the house and caught a cat stretching out its front paw into the pack'n'play. Emma had tears streaming down her face.

"Don't worry," Mrs. Hodges said. "It's just Oscar. He's harmless. Come on, Oscar, pussy. Come to Mommy."

"Oh, Emma, it's okay." Julia picked up Emma and stood near the front window. The cleaning truck was just pulling onto the street. "Mrs. Hodges, the cleaning crew is here. I need to go out to meet them."

"Give me Emma," Mrs. Hodges said. "It's too hot for her out there."

Julia hesitated but handed her child over to the woman. Mrs. Hodges reached into Julia's baby bag and pulled out juice and crackers. Emma looked content.

Julia made her way to the truck. "Hi, I'm Mrs. Edwards. I'm glad you made it."

"Yes, ma'am."

"If you find any drug paraphernalia, will you please let me know? My neighbor tells me that our former tenants may have used this place as a drug house. I don't want any surprises while I'm living here."

"My boss will call you with a full report of what we find."

"I'd appreciate that."

Emma was babbling as Mrs. Hodges fed her lunch at the kitchen table.

"We shouldn't be taking up so much of your time," Julia said, sitting next to them.

"Nonsense. I have all sorts of time. Besides, I wanted to show you a few more things in my garden."

"It might start raining." Julia glanced outside.

"I have a stroller that I use for my grandchild. I'll get it."

Julia smiled at Emma. Acquiescing to the older woman felt odd. Mrs. Hodges pushed the stroller into the kitchen.

Mrs. Hodges picked up Emma and sat her in the stroller. "She's a heavy girl."

Julia smiled. "Eleven months now. They're pretty heavy at that age."

Mrs. Hodges led the way to the far corner of her yard. Under the large tree sat a wooden bench with an inscription. Julia stepped up and read it to herself ...

> Underneath lies our dear cat, Benjie,
> Who died cruelly at the hands of
> Villains who shall remain unnamed.

Julia took a step back and sighed. "What happened to Benjie?"

Mrs. Hodges took in a deep breath and let it out slowly. "Never quite sure. One morning we found him strung up by his neck under this tree. Strangled. The neighbor boys used to taunt him. We never had proof of what actually happened."

Julia gasped. "How awful!"

"Yes. It was. Let's move from here down to a nicer spot," Mrs. Hodges said.

They walked over to a patch of light pink, red, purple, and black roses that seemed to all be on one bush.

Julia chuckled. "How unusual."

"I grafted them. Put them together as a memorial to Loretta and Elroy. They represent the hope that had gone bad in their lives."

Julia allowed her mind to wander as she searched for a reply. "What a thoughtful gesture."

"I thought so." Mrs. Hodges stood and glanced around with a look of satisfaction written on her face.

Julia wondered how often she had showed off her handiwork to others. "Is there anything else you wanted me to see?"

Snapping out of a reverie, Mrs. Hodges replied, "Oh yes, something very important. Follow me."

They stepped up to a patch of magnificent, blood-red roses. The blooms were larger than any of the others in the yard. The foliage was a vivid green.

"These are my favorite," Mrs. Hodges said. "I imported them myself from Germany. They're my babies. You understand, of course?" She glared at Emma for just a second before scanning Julia for a reaction. "What it is to have a baby ... something so important that you spend all your time nurturing, feeding, caring. I spend all my time with these roses every day. I talk to them and coax them through inclement weather. Pick off insects. So many things to do." She laughed. "Such a troublesome time protecting them from harm." She glanced over at the house. "Isn't much distance between their flowerbed and your yard. Things that grow in your yard are always encroaching into mine. Down through the soil and into my yard. The worst is that nasty poison ivy!"

"Oh?" Julia glanced around.

Mrs. Hodges glared at Julia. "Did you know that I'm highly allergic to poison ivy? I must wear gloves to garden, and very long gloves. Even then, my entire system gets sick. When I'm sick, I'm prevented from tending to my garden. How do you think that makes me feel?"

"Oh?" Julia frowned.

The woman's tone softened. "I'm going to need your help."

"My help?"

Mrs. Hodges nodded. "Your help in keeping the poison ivy from your yard creeping into mine. Do you think you'll be able to do that?"

Julia's eyes widened. "Mrs. Hodges, I am sorry."

Emma screeched from the stroller and flailed her arms.

Julia picked up her daughter and smiled. "We must go. I'm so grateful for the tour. Really I am."

The thunder rumbled and big droplets fell. Julia hurried through the kitchen and grabbed the pack'n'play before darting out of the house. She glanced back to see Mrs. Hodges peering out of her window with arms folded across her chest. She seemed to be smiling. A smile of smugness, triumphant.

When the cleaning crew had finished, Julia drove to Adam's office. It was pouring rain now. There were so many questions and she needed answers. Shaking off the wet, she placed a sleeping Emma on Adam's couch and covered her with a blanket.

A knock on the door grabbed her attention. Not wanting to wake Emma, she opened it only a crack. An attractive young woman with flaming red hair smiled. With one hand on her hip, she used the other to push the door open. She looked inside the office.

"Is Adam here?" the woman asked.

"No. He has a class right now. Can I help you?"

"Would you tell him I stopped by?"

"Any message?"

"No. Just tell him Amanda came by."

Amanda performed a quick pivot and flounced down the hallway. Julia wasn't sure if the woman noticed Emma or even cared if she had. Something dark was starting to sprout inside Julia, and no apology could erase it. His father. Her father too. And after the promises. After that first time before Emma was born. Now the anger was there, but it tasted nasty, more bitter. It was a poison that was spreading through her. She had the steel to push it out of her mind and simply tend to the business at hand. She sat and pushed a number into her phone.

The first call was to the cleaning company. "This is Mrs. Edwards. Did you receive the report from your crew at Granger Avenue?"

"Just had it put on my desk, ma'am."

"And?"

"Let me see ... trash and leftover food, dog hair, urine, cigarettes, and paper waste."

"Any evidence of drugs?"

"No, ma'am. Says it looked like only one bedroom was ever used. No evidence of illegal activity. No evidence of alcohol use."

"Thank you." Julia was not sure what to make of the information. Next, she called the local police department.

"Hi, my name is Julia Edwards. I'm the new owner at 2040 Granger Avenue. My husband and I had rented the property for about a year and we're moving into it now. For our safety, I wanted to know if there were any reports of drug activity, poisoning, or malicious harming of animals at this location?"

The officer chuckled. "Lots of questions, ma'am. Give me a sec …"

Julia could hear the man typing. She glanced over at Emma and smiled. The child was still asleep.

"No drugs, ma'am. A poisoning was reported but wasn't considered criminal, just an accident. The dead animal was never solved. Would need an inquest to determine the cause of death, and we don't do that with pets. That's all I have. Good neighborhood, ma'am."

Julia sat down her phone. She was relieved that there was nothing to the drugs. But what about what Mrs. Hodges had said? She turned to the computer and clicked it on. She waited the few minutes until it loaded. Then, in the search engine, she typed in "Cynthia Roscoe, cause of death."

Just a few random hits. An obituary with the date of death. May 18, 1960 … age thirty. Survived by spouse, John Roscoe, and daughter, Rose, age three. She scrolled to a newspaper article that featured the woman's death. It stated that she had started a bonfire in her yard. The pile contained poison ivy. Her husband was away on business, and the daughter was asleep. Cynthia tended the fire until it burned out. Unaware that it contained the poison ivy, she sat breathing in the fumes. Later that night, she had a severe allergic reaction that shut down her lungs. By morning, she had stopped breathing. The child found her and sat by her side until the father returned the following day.

Why did Mrs. Hodges' father say that her mother was murdered by burglars? Julia thought about it for a long time and then she understood.

The moving van had emptied the contents and placed the furniture where Julia or Adam had directed. When Adam shut the front door, Julia took an exhausted Emma to her crib. In the master bedroom, she glanced out the window for only a moment before shutting the blinds. Mrs. Hodges had a habit of staring out her windows. Julia motioned for Adam to sit with her on the bed.

"We need to talk about our neighbor," Julia said.

"What about our neighbor?"

"We need to be nice to her. I think she's trouble."

"It's just a fluke that you spent that much time at her house. You owe her nothing."

"I feel involved," Julia replied.

"You're not involved. You probably know more than you should. She's not a friend or your responsibility."

Julia nodded. "Perhaps you are right."

After dinner, Adam opened the door. He reached down and picked up a small, potted rose with a note:

```
Welcome to the neighborhood,

This is a cutting from the Cynthia
Roscoe Rose. Plant it along the fence
in the back.

Good fences make good neighbors.
```

Mel and Rose Hodges

Julia stepped up and Adam handed her the note. She read it over and sighed. "See, she won't let me go."

"Don't be silly. It's just a friendly, neighborly gesture."

Julia kept after her husband to check the fence for poison ivy. Neither knew much about gardening. Not certain that they could recognize it, they studied the pesty plant on the internet. It looked one way in the fall and another in the spring.

Julia tried to avoid going to her yard when Mrs. Hodges was tending her roses. The woman kept to a schedule of early morning watering and early afternoon de-weeding.

It was late afternoon when Julia took Emma out to her swing. Mrs. Hodges stepped out from the shadows on the opposite side of her yard. She was dressed from head to toe in white linen. A veil covered her face, and she wore gloves that ran up to her elbows. She strode to the fence and screamed out, "Do you know what you've done?"

Julia froze.

Mrs. Hodges didn't wait for an answer. "You have allowed your poison ivy to crawl into my roses. I told you to take care of it. Now, I have it on my arms and I've been sick. My husband must tend to my roses. You are thoughtless and cruel!" She turned and marched up her back steps.

Julia sighed. *I refuse to cower in my own home!* She called a fencing company. Within three days, a five-foot, opaque fence was erected between their yard and the Hodges. She knew it would probably affect the light to Mrs. Hodges' roses. But that couldn't be helped. Mrs. Hodges could transplant them if she wanted. But the fence would solve the poison ivy problem. A three-foot deep trench along the fence line killed everything that was growing.

Julia instructed the company to put poison ivy killer along the line for good measure. She also told the company to place the yard debris in a pile near the rear of her yard. She would take care of bagging it in a few days. They told her to be careful of the poison ivy because it remained dangerous. She said she would be.

Two weeks later, Julia asked Adam to burn the trash pile after she and Emma had gone to bed, and to tend to it until the fire extinguished itself.

-77-

Do You Know Your Neighbors?

Lynn's thoughts …

This story makes me want to sing a commercial jingle … *like a good neighbor …*

What is the definition of a good neighbor? And is this story about being a good neighbor, or is it about marriage and a broken promise?

When I finished reading, I had to sit back and think a little. I was so centered on this weird neighbor that I was too concerned over whether she was a little *off* or not. Then it hit me. The neighbor knew that the husband was cheating. And to help out the wife, planted an idea to rid her of the problem. Maybe she was a great neighbor after all.

What makes a great writer? Someone who can tell a story without actually saying the words. They allude to something. And that is what we find in this short story. An odd lady, who instead of coming right out in the open and stating that the husband is a cheat, alluded to it. Then, instead of telling the wife how she could kill her husband, she simply guided her to a sad story about how burning poison ivy can be deadly. How sad.

The short note about how fences make good neighbors had nothing to do with being a good neighbor. It was a hint as to where to find the ivy that would do the deed. And the idea of revenge was displayed proudly on a backyard bench.

I'll have to remember this. We should never get mad … just get even.

Do You Know Your Neighbors?

Enlightenment

Sue Ellen Russell

I wiped my sweaty palms down my white, silk pants. The ones that matched my black-and-white checkered jacket. I stopped myself before I left a permanent stain. Instead, I raised my head and gazed out at the hostile crowd that was waiting for me to explain why the Board decided to allow our teachers to include racial equity in our history classes.

As they shifted in their chairs, I stood. Even though I worked for a progressive, suburban school district, the loudest protests seemed to be coming from the middle class, white parents whose sanitized education differed from what was taught at our school. The sea of angry faces echoed images from the sixties of those battling desegregation. Did they know how they looked, or did they even care?

The few people of color who sat straight in their chairs remained quiet, wearing a defiant expression. I guess their family histories told a different type of story. Then again, inside our district, only about thirty percent of the students were black. As I walked to the podium, parents held placards above their heads …

SAY NO TO CRITICAL RACE THEORY

… with the letters CRT in the middle of a circle with a slash through it …

EDUCATION NOT INDOCTRINATION

… one of my favorites, and the one that made me smile …

CREATING RACIAL TENSION

The parents knew my stance, for it had already been reported in the news. Someone had thrown a rock at my window, and threats were yelled from honking cars. Now I wondered if anyone here were responsible for the harassment. Boos and hisses greeted me as I leaned toward the microphone. I waited until they calmed down.

"If you will oblige me …" I said, talking over a few remaining instigators. "I have one question to ask."

The voices stilled as it registered that I hadn't launched into a scholastic defense of our curriculum. A spark of curiosity flashed across a few eyes.

"With apologies to the people of color in the audience, who will answer my question?" No one moved. "How many of you would become black if you could?"

A woman from the front shook her head and answered, "What does that have to do with anything?"

I smiled. "It has everything to do with it. If I had a magic wand and could change you from a white woman to a black one, would you do it?"

The woman sat back and frowned.

I glanced around at the others who remained quiet. "Anyone else? Anyone at all?"

The silence grew and my nerves thickened. "That just about sums it up." I shook my head and stepped away from the podium. As I left the room, I nodded over at the board members.

Marissa sat in the second row and allowed her eyes to linger on the departing board member. *Liz, I believe that was her name.* She glanced back at the angry or shocked faces before allowing the door to close behind her. Of course, these people understood why no one in the audience raised their hand at her question. Most never had to worry about the effects of negative stereotyping on them or their children. They never thought about the news stories that covered the attendance of a senator or member of Congress who met with racist nationalists behind our backs. Or how public outcries about taking down a Confederate flag or removing a Confederate statue felt when these things were created with the sole purpose of intimidating people of color.

Marissa glanced down at her phone and re-read the news article. Just that morning, a white couple had stabbed a black man for no reason other than the color of his skin. She knew too well how the voices of angry citizens about the uncomfortable racial issues were raised, and how they exhausted people of color who understood but dare not speak, for their objections were code for African Americans not knowing their place.

Marissa looked over at the few quiet parents and nodded. Did they want her to speak up for them? As they nodded back as a signal of encouragement, she sighed and smoothed out her skirt. When the Chair asked for comments from the audience, Marissa stood.

The Chair nodded, and as she approached the lectern, the back of her neck burned, as though the barrage of hostile eyes that fell upon her emitted actual flames. She kept her head held high and moved through the attendees, trying to ignore the murmuring. She waited while the Chair held up his hand for silence. As the voices dwindled, she steadied her breathing.

Marissa glanced at the section where the protesting parents were sitting. Then, in a loud and clear voice she stated, "I didn't have to raise my hand because I live with who I am every day. My color may not be the first thing I think of when I wake, but I'm reminded of it when I leave my house. A common theme I hear, and one that I heard just now, is that learning about our country's racial history will make children uncomfortable."

She glanced around at the nodding heads and dug her nails deeper into her hands to remain calm.

"Not only is critical race theory not taught in high school, but my children are made to feel uncomfortable by people just like you. Like me, they're reminded that *you* matter and *we* don't."

She gestured to the signs a few of the parents held.

"Those signs make children uncomfortable. Hateful expressions make children uncomfortable. Whose children are we talking about protecting? Because it damn sure doesn't seem like anyone wants to protect mine."

The friends from her section near the front stood and clapped, and to her surprise, so did several of the other parents in the back. And, near the hall, several students cheered. The noise drowned out the objections of the parents holding the signs.

Liz stepped back inside and clapped. She nodded directly at Marissa and smiled.

As she returned to her seat amid the continued clapping, a tear wet Melissa's cheek. Despite everything, she loved this country, and maybe, just maybe, some of *it* would somehow love her back.

Enlightenment

Lynn's thoughts …

This story touched my heart in so many ways. At first, I was taken back a little, but after reading it several times, I could relate from where the message was stemming.

I taught law at a local college for over ten years and loved it. My biggest challenge was motivating my students to *read* and *retain* what they had learned. One way to wake them up was to bring in the most controversial topics I could find. Make the right side fight with the left and the front fight with the back. Then, in the end, the conclusion was simple …

There is no right or wrong answer to anything.

If I could imprint that one thought into their brains, then I had succeeded. To understand that every problem, every question, every thought possessed various answers and solutions, could be a difficult concept to grasp. If we make some people happy over here, others over there will be upset and vice versa. Therefore, what is the final solution?

Critical Race Theory (CRT) has been around since the 1960's. Not many realize that. They believe it is a new concept, which it is not. On one side, we have the emotional view where we must take care of others. On the other side, we have the view where we all must learn how to care for ourselves. Why can't we just stand in the middle and give help where help is needed and teach at the same time? Why can't we just treat people as people? Why must we count melanin? I often wonder if someday our melanin percentages will be proudly or shamefully displayed on our driver's licenses or foreheads. I believe they have a supplement for that, actually … available on Amazon.

But here is the problem. If everyone was the same color, the same skin tone, would that solve the problem? Or would we find something else to weigh in on?

# Good Neighbor Policy

Drury Wellford

Patty lived in the duplex next to Hank's for about five years. While painting her living room, Hank introduced himself by saying that her handyman was making too much noise. Therefore, after so many years, she fully understood that Hank could be nasty, and she vowed to do everything she could to stay away from his bad side.

Her children came home for the holidays and were outside smoking and drinking.

At precisely eleven, Hank opened his bedroom window and yelled. "It's *too* late for that kind of racket. Y'all go on inside!"

The children had not woken Patty, but Hank's yelling definitely did.

It would be almost daylight when Hank would lumber painfully down his stairs. Time for his daily routine with an early-morning breakfast at the local diner. Just like clockwork, the morning stomping woke her. Hank was old, but he never looked stiff when he wandered out to his car. In fact, he looked rather spry for his age. Too spry to stair stomp.

Once the *rules* were set between them, Hank often greeted her with a chipper, "Good mawnin', how you?" and usually at the most unfortunate of moments. Mostly when she was leaving for work and couldn't avoid him. She wanted to flip him the bird on numerous occasions, but instead, responded with an equally sugary, "I'm fine, how you?" or "The weather's looking good."

One time, she spied him sitting in a matinee at the local theater. He was dressed in his routine faded, red T-shirt, frazzled khaki pants, and beaten-up deck shoes. He looked like a shriveled-up turtle. She had heard from their gossipy neighbors that he had retired from teaching history at the county school. She wondered why he dressed so sloppy, even if it was just the movies. It surprised her seeing him there, and she walked by acting like she hadn't noticed him.

She was glad her children never had him for a teacher, based on how much he screamed.

A time came when it seemed like Hank had gone away. His car was parked in his designated space, but the early-morning step-stomping had stopped. Instead, things were eerily quiet until later in the day when she heard what sounded like a young person's feet racing up and down his stairs. The sounds of hectic activity, such as changing of bed sheets or vacuuming, echoed through her walls. A rat-a-tat-tat on Hank's door every late afternoon seemed odd. Hank was an early-to-bed and early-to-rise type, so it seemed like this visitor might make Hank stay up a bit later than normal.

Then it all started to make sense. The footsteps must have belonged to a home care worker. Could Hank be sick? He was in his eighties. She felt sorry for the nurse. Afterall, they were not assisting the nicest man in the world.

She thought about taking over some home-baked food now that he was sick and couldn't make his own dinner. It would be a nice thing for a neighbor to do. The more she thought about it, the more she thought it best to not become involved. If they found him dead, so be it. It would be what the Good Lord intended.

The last time she actually saw Hank, she had just locked herself out of her unit. Feeling stressed and confused, she didn't know what to do.

She stared at Hank's door and thought, *This is the person I should be able to trust an extra key with in times of emergencies. But if he did have an extra key and I knocked, would he even answer?* Patty was sure he probably wouldn't, or if he did, it would be an irritating experience.

She looked in her secret hiding place on the inside of the patio fence. But no key. Her adult children must have used it and forgotten to put it back.

"Shit."

She fell to her knees beside the fence and reached under in hopes that it might have fallen from the nail. No need to pay hundreds to hire a locksmith if she didn't have to.

Just as her arm squeezed into the small opening, Hank waddled to his car with his turtle-like head perched atop his collarless and faded, red T-shirt. The ugliest clothes for a man his age.

Was he or wasn't he sick?

He watched as Patty squeezed her arm under the fence. He nodded from his car and said, "Good mawnin'. How you?"

"Locked myself out," Patty said, barely able to turn her head to look at him.

Hank waved while holding up his car key. "Have a nice day."

Patty finally gave up and asked a pedestrian if she could use their cell to call a locksmith. The pedestrian was sympathetic and full of wonderful advice.

"You should leave an extra key with your neighbor, or in a secret hiding place. That's what I do. The locksmith's gonna cost."

Patty thanked them for their advice, not wanting to go into detail of the missing key or living next to a shitty neighbor named Hank. And yeah, she knew the locksmith was going to fleece her, but what else could she do?

As she waited outside in the glaring sunlight and high humidity of a mid-August morning, she reviewed her resentments about the whole situation. Hank was just a tired, old turd. That was the problem. She liked her privacy and didn't want neighbors all up in her business. But she'd be more than happy to keep an extra key for Hank if he'd keep one for her.

Why did he have to be such a pill? And who did he think he was, yelling at her kids? And why did he have to wake her every morning with his loud stomping?

She never complained to him about it, but maybe she should. She'd let him know that she owned an unpleasant side too. A side that was permanently directed at him.

So what if he's a sick, old man? He better not expect anything from me!

In fact, she was inclined to write him a letter and tell him that, because he was so mean, he'd cost her three hundred in locksmith services.

Patty's rage lasted until she watched his car pull into his parking space with the locksmith behind him. Hank got out and looked at the man. He waddled around the corner to his door and slipped into his unit just like a vampire.

The locksmith worked on her door and filled her with advice. "Why don't you leave a key with that guy? Then you won't have to waste money on me."

He was nice, but Patty wanted him to just shut up and get the damn door open.

Many months later and on a rainy Saturday morning, Patty snuggled in her bed and listened to Hank's stomping. She froze when a distinct sound of him falling, while shouting out a slight whoop, gave her chills. Then, nothing but dead silence filled the air.

She rolled over and drifted back to sleep, soothed by the rhythm of the rain.

Lynn's thoughts …

The Hatfields and McCoys fought back in the 1860's and ended in one of the largest and most political trials of US history. Therefore, if the courts couldn't stop the Hatfields and McCoys from fighting, then perhaps there is no hope for the rest of us, and neighbors will continue to feud until the end of time.

It's interesting how someone's habits can become so annoying that we honestly do not care if that individual is alive or dead. Could it be that we sense a little negative something within ourselves, which then makes us work twice as hard to destroy?

Our author does a wonderful job of bringing to light how we have a tendency to be our own worst enemies. If Patty had simply taken the time to become … neighborly … then they could have shared keys, and she could have saved herself a lot of time and money. Then again, perhaps feeling annoyed at someone gives us a little nudge of power that we would not normally have.

Now that Hank has fallen down the stairs, who will Patty leave her key with? And … who's to say that her next neighbor wouldn't be a little worse.

- 94 -

Having Words

Micaela Meder

"You honestly have the gall to come to my party dressed as a cereal box?"

Jim's eyes narrowed and he shifted as much as he could while wearing the large contraption. Praying not to lose his balance and fall off the porch, he raised his chin and shook the plastic knife at Evan.

"A cereal box with anger issues, even." Evan nodded.

Jim frowned as he took a deeper breath. Glaring at his friend, he replied, "I'm a *cereal* killer. Hence, the cereal box and knife. As in serial killer but —"

"Okay!" Evan raised his hands as if to surrender. "I get it. I do."

Jim huffed and poked the tip of the plastic knife into Evan's ribs a few inches below the imitation sheriff's badge. Evan stepped aside so that the cardboard box would fit through the entryway.

Lisa and Mandy, dressed in their own costumes and eating potato chips, waved.

"By the way, your twin arrived ages ago and is sulking on the deck." Evan reclaimed his seat on the couch and placed his arm over Lisa's shoulders.

"Even on a good day ..." – Jim frowned – "... Steve considers me to be an embarrassment. Therefore, on a day such as today ... he's twice as disgusted at the thought of being seen with me ... in public."

Evan nodded.

Mandy, dressed as a colorful anime character, sat cross-legged in front of the couch and giggled. Pressing her knuckles to her chin as if imitating thoughtfulness, she glanced up at Jim. "And you are what exactly?"

The pair of cat ears sitting in Lisa's hair leaned as she tilted her head. The painted whiskers made her amazement resemble a curious cat.

Jim sighed. "Seriously, people? I'm a *cereal* killer. It's not that difficult to figure out."

The girls rolled their eyes and smiled. "Of course." They chorused together.

Evan laughed. "You're not fashionably late, so I'll let your choice of costume slide."

"Late? Darn. And here I wanted to be punctual." Jim grinned unrepentantly at the pained groans and grins that inevitably followed.

"NO!" A loud voice echoed in from the back deck. "I said ... no more puns!" Pounding footsteps bounced off the walls.

Jim understood. It was time to leave. "Uh-oh." He wrestled his way out of the cereal box and raced out the front door with his twin not far behind.

"No puns!" his brother yelled, flailing his arms.

Whose stupid idea was it to go camping so early in the spring? Jim would have to cuff them upside the head once his fingers were no longer resembling a block of ice.

The twins scoured the surrounding woodland for sticks and branches suitable for kindling. Steve and Jim worked in peaceful coordination for a while, although they struggled to find that which wasn't damp from the recent rains. Jim managed to find one short and dry branch – a miracle in itself – but Steve was not having any luck.

"Hey," Steve said, pointing to a pile of leaves at the foot of a tree. "Do yah reckon there could be some dry sticks under there?"

Jim shivered and blew on his fingers as his breath fogged in the air. "Could be, I guess."

Steve dug into the leaves. When it became clear that the only reward for his efforts would be numb, wet hands, he sat back and sighed.

"Let's keep searching. Just leaf it." As soon as he said the words, Jim regretted not having a filter. "I mean ... let's just branch out to cover more area!"

His brother stiffened and slowly stood. Steve' leveling glare seemed frightening.

Acting on instinct and wanting to be within his twin's good graces, Jim held out his one piece of kindling. "Would you like to have this one instead?"

Lisa, Evan, and Mandy warmed themselves by the small fire. The twins were just taking too long and they were cold.

Harried footfalls filled the air as Jim darted into the clearing and tripped. He raised the single stick and whispered, "Firewood?"

"Is that all you found?" Evan asked.

Steve walked out from the tree line glaring at his twin.

The three friends said nothing.

"Honestly, only one stick that isn't wet," Jim said, brushing himself off. "We couldn't even find two, let alone tree."

Mandy and Lisa giggled.

Jim risked a glance at his twin.

"Excuse me while I toss my disappointment of a brother into the campfire," Steve said as he took in a deep breath. He stepped toward his brother.

"Not fair. I only let a couple of puns slip and now I'm ..." His eyes widened and he made a small keening sound as he desperately tried to hold the next two words back. "Under fire?" Jim covered his mouth to hide his laugh.

Steve balled his hands into fists.

Jim found the next words bubbling up from the back of his throat. He knew better, but he just had to say it. "I think that in a hot second this situation is going to get heated with Steve all fired up. He's practically burning with rage, and can someone just stop me, please?"

Evan reached over and covered Jim's mouth with his hand. An uneasy silence hovered over the burning embers.

Steve took in a deeper breath and stated firmly, "No more puns!"

Jim's high-pitched shriek echoed throughout the clearing as he darted into the trees with his twin close behind.

It was such a scorcher of a day, and Jim was sure he was melting. After helping his brother prepare some wraps for lunch, he seated himself in front of the fan.

Steve beamed as he added the final bits of filling with dramatic flair and stepped back to admire his work. "Done!"

"It's a wrap, people!" Jim said, clapping his hands. His jubilant mood died when Steve snarled.

After entering the house, Evan, Lisa, and Mandy sighed at the reprieve from the relentless heat.

"Where's Jim?" Mandy asked as they dug into the wraps that were now on the dining table.

No reply.

"Steve?" Evan prompted.

A gleam darkened in Steve's eyes and he smirked. Calmly and slowly, he picked up his drink and walked toward the sliding door. He paused only briefly and just long enough to reply, "Don't worry. He's just been banished from the delightfully air-conditioned indoors as a ... pun-ishment!"

A silence followed, broken only by Jim's indignant cry from somewhere in the backyard. "You just punned, dear brother. Come out here, you hypocritical punk!"

Lynn's thoughts …

To pun or not to pun, now that is the question. My first experience with a pun was reading a Piers Anthony novel, *A Spell for Chameleon*. Within the pages, we meet Bink. A young man who lacks a magical capability, which means he would be banned from Xanth. While waiting for the court's verdict, Bink poured out his heart to his parents' bedpost and soon learned more about his parents than he wanted to know. Piers took the – *between you, me, and the bedpost* – idiom to a higher level.

Being the joker of a group can be fun, although the lack of reality will become old, and that individual's attitude will fade and dissolve into the nuisance section.

Irritation … indignation … anger … any of these sound familiar? I can honestly say that, on a weekly basis, I am stating several times that one of the children who live here is being quite annoying.

Perhaps that is where the word punishment actually comes from. In reality, to inflict a penalty as a retribution does fit. While analyzing this story, I kept falling back to the *cereal killer* and what the author was trying to portray. Then it hit me. A killer is punished for their crime. Therefore, wouldn't a pun abuser be punished for theirs? I felt it an interesting analogy. And I found it clever for the author to use a costume as an example.

Lindsey Hobson

The road was calling to me again. A familiar pull that I hadn't felt for a while. I had lived here longer than anywhere. For some strange reason, it was always easy for me to leave. Anything I'd ever need still fit inside one suitcase.

For me, it was always about the trip. The open roads that intertwined with my most intimate thoughts were all that I ever wanted. This time, however, I knew where I was headed, and my thoughts felt jumbled and heavy. I made the two-day drive stretch into four, savoring what was likely my last road trip. Even with the extra time to prepare, I was not ready when I pulled into the driveway.

During the thirty-some years that I had been away, it was obvious that the house was never without visitors. Discarded beer cans and miscellaneous trash littered the yard. Vines snaked under the eaves where nature constantly tried to take it all back. I had no idea why I kept this place. Then again, who'd want to buy it?

It was smaller than I remembered … if that were even possible. The door was unlocked and barely clung to its hinges. I peeked in the room that I had once shared with my sister, Sue Ellen. The double bed was still there, and the rusted springs still stuck haphazardly from the bare mattress.

During the long and cold winter nights, we'd huddle together and watch as our breaths made clouds above our heads. In the summertime, it would feel so hot that our bare skin stuck together whenever we touched. But … there was comfort during those years, even when it was uncomfortable. I wondered why it took me so long to realize that.

Outside, the sun was sinking behind the knob. It always became dark in this valley before anywhere else, as if the world were in a hurry to hide our shack and broken-down vehicles.

I suddenly realized that I was bone tired, as if I had walked all those miles that it took to get here. Climbing back into my car, I reclined the seat and was out before I could start counting sheep.

I woke early to the songs of birds. Despite my cramped sleeping quarters, I felt well rested. The house looked even worse in the early morning light. Graffiti covered the walls, and it was evident that animals had been living here. The house, if one would still call it that, was beyond repair. Trying to salvage it was not on my agenda. I was just here to write.

I had tried writing my memoir for several years to no avail. However, as soon as I crossed that threshold, the words came rushing in. After clearing a space on the floor, I pulled out my notebook and pen.

I was born the third and youngest child of Clyde and Suzette Mooney, a miner and a housewife, respectively. My mother quit school at sixteen and was raising three children by the time she was twenty. Not much can be said about my childhood. We were poor and I always knew I wanted to get away.

My older brother, Billy, followed in my father's footsteps and became a miner. He died when a shaft collapsed just a month after he started work. Billy was a bully, and only Mama was sad. Daddy died in a car crash a year later. He was a mean drunk, and no one – least of all Mama – was sad. My older sister, Sue Ellen, married a dentist when she was nineteen. He was thirty-nine. I wanted to leave home, too, but Mama got sick, so I stayed until she passed. I was twenty-three and had the whole world at my feet.

Oh, Mama. She lived her entire life beaten down by others, and when she finally had a chance to live for herself, cancer snuck in and beat her down even harder. I lived my life for myself all because of her. Never once had I allowed another or anything to hold me back.

Some people think I'm selfish. Maybe I am. Most of my friends married their high school sweethearts right after graduation and had kids who grew up to be just like them. They were living the humble life, but that was not the life for me.

I came close to marrying once. He was the pilot, and I was the stewardess. A smooth talker. He almost caught me, but I caught him first — with another member of the crew. I pawned the ring and bought a one-way ticket, feeling relieved to have dodged that bullet.

After that, I toured the world. Literally. All the touristy spots like Paris, Rome, Greece — but also, the hidden places. A secret beach in Bali that only the locals knew about. A dark bar in Delhi, or places girls from small towns did not normally find themselves in.

When my growling stomach could no longer be ignored, I put down my pen and paper. I hadn't eaten since I splurged on room service the day before. Glancing around, I realized I was in desperate need of supplies. Especially if I was going to stay inside this house.

A few fast-food restaurants now dotted the road into town. But their neon signs wouldn't hide the empty, weed-choked storefronts that surrounded them. I passed a sign informing me that the Church of Christ welcomes me to White Oak, and another that was proudly displaying a football win from twenty-five years ago.

Hank's Grocery seemed a likely place to find what I needed. So, I pulled into the lot and parked. I was greeted by a blast of cold air as the automatic doors slid open. The store was almost deserted, just as I was hoping it would be. Produce was out of the question since I had no way to keep it fresh. I loaded up on the middle-of-the-store stuff that healthy people were supposed to avoid.

"Adelle St. Claire? Is that you?! OH … MY … GOD!"

I flinched and took in a deep breath, wondering if I could pretend to be hard of hearing. The click-click-click of heels against the aging linoleum told me there was no hope of escape.

"I can't believe this! I'm like your biggest fan."

I faked a smile. "Thank you."

"*The Stranger* is my absolute favorite book ever."

"Thank you." For the first time in my life, I was at a loss for words.

"What are you doing in White Oak?"

"I grew up here."

"Really? I never read that in any of your bios. I figured you were from … oh, I don't know, maybe … New York, or some other big and exciting place."

"I've been away for a long time. At least it feels that way. Excuse me, I was just going to check out."

"Oh, sure. I'm the cashier. I'll take you right up here."

I didn't have half of what I needed. Nor would I ever have thought that high heels were the preferred choice of a Hank's Grocery clerk.

"Are you working on a new novel?" she asked as she rang up my few items.

"Sort of. I'm working on a memoir."

"Oh? How exciting." She gushed with excitement. "I can't wait to read it!"

"Thank you," I repeated for the third time in as many minutes. "If we could keep this our little secret that would be great. I just want to focus on my work."

"Gotcha, totally …" She made an elaborate showing of locking her lips with an imaginary key and tossing it over her shoulder.

I took my grocery bags out to my car, knowing full well that every one of the 1,593 residents of White Oak would soon know that I was here.

I surveyed my purchases – bottled water, granola bars, crackers, tuna, and Vienna sausages. Before I could decide on which packaged meat to eat, the sound of crunching gravel filled my ears.

News still traveled fast around here. "Thanks, Stilettos."

I'd recognize Sue Ellen anywhere. Even though it had been decades since I'd last seen her. She was still beautiful as ever. I stood on the broken front steps and smiled. "Hello, Sue Ellen."

"The rumors are true then," she said a little coldly. "The famous Adelle Mooney ... sorry, St. Claire is back in town. I had to see it for myself."

I flinched at her tone but she continued.

"Thirty years, Adelle. Thirty years and never a card or a call. Never a visit. Why'd you come back? Why now?"

"Cancer." I blurted it out so fast that I surprised myself. I had meant to keep it a secret, but she just looked so angry, so hurt.

Her perfectly constructed facade of indifference vanished. She ran up and wrapped her arms around me. We were kids again, huddled together inside the warm blankets of our double bed.

"I'm sorry, Dell," she whispered. She held me at arm's length and looked me over so intently that I wondered if she could see the illness inside of me.

I shrugged. "I don't know why I came back."

"Come home with me," she said and her voice sounded a little whiny. "Bob passed away last year. The kids are gone. It's just me in that big, old house."

"No, no, I can't impose." I took a step back. "It's been too long."

"Nonsense." Her voice was loud and firm. She grabbed my hand and looked around. "God, I haven't been back here in ages."

"You haven't missed much. But the place is more disgusting than it used to be, and that's saying something."

"Oh, Dell, it wasn't that bad," she replied. It was the same 'ol optimistic Sue. "Remember the tree? I wonder if it's still there?"

She pulled me around the house and into the backyard. Shading my eyes with my free hand, I looked up and could still see them. Several pieces of cloth tied to the lower branches. They were faded now, but I knew what each one was. A piece of fabric from a new-to-us Easter dress. A strip of Christmas ribbon from the doll Sue had saved up to buy me. A bow from a prom dress worn first by her, and later by me. We tied a part of anything good to that tree, so when times were bad, we could look at it and remember.

There was a newer one that I didn't recognize. I stepped closer and stared at it.

"My wedding dress," she whispered.

Old habits die hard.

Sue Ellen's house was elegant, just like her. The walls were filled with photographs of babies, children, and families. I knew she was watching me while I searched through the familiar faces.

"They're beautiful," I said. "How exciting it must have been ... to raise all of these kids."

"Not nearly as exciting as yours."

"Perhaps. I mean, I did have plenty of adventures. But now I wonder if I made the wrong choices. You're surrounded with people that care about you. I'm surrounded with miles of empty ocean."

"I would give anything to have just one of your adventures. Just one."

She pulled a large album from off the bookcase and handed it to me. I opened it and read through the articles that I had written for various newspapers years ago. That was when I still went by the name Adelle Mooney. Articles about me when I became a bestselling author and changed my name to Adelle St. Claire filled the other pages. She had everything I had ever written and everything ever written about me.

"I don't know what to say." I felt speechless for the second time in a day.

"We may not have kept in touch, but I kept tabs on you." She frowned. "Why never a letter? Never return home?"

"Stubbornness perhaps?" I sighed. "I wanted so desperately to get away, and then when I did, I worked as a stewardess and experienced the world. I started writing abroad for various papers and later my novels. I never wanted to come back, and after a while, I felt like I couldn't. Why didn't you ever contact me?"

"Stubbornness perhaps?" She smiled but the creases didn't reach her eyes. "I wanted out of there just as much as you did. When I met Bob, I thought that he was my ticket. I was in love and busied myself with his three kids. After we had three of our own, I thought about contacting you but kept putting it off … maybe I was a little jealous."

"Jealous of what?"

"Your glamorous life? Then it just felt as if it was too late."

We remained quiet for a while. Each lost in her own thoughts.

"How about dinner?" she said. "You must be starving."

I nodded. "Famished."

Word spread quickly about the famous writer staying at Sue Ellen Page's house. We received so many visitors that we lost count. People we went to school with. Kids of people we went to school with. I laughed more than I had laughed in a long time.

She only asked about the cancer once.

"Can't anything be done?" she whispered.

"I refused treatment. I couldn't stand the thought of being poked and prodded for the rest of my life. I demand to live and die on my terms. Not some doctor's."

She accepted my decision, albeit reluctantly. "How long do you have?"

"Maybe a year."

I had never doubted my decision until now. Now, I wished I had more time.

For a while, we busied ourselves with her garden or taking long walks. She taught me how to make jam, and I taught her how to make my favorite Indian dish. We never looked at the calendar that she kept on her kitchen wall.

But I could feel myself becoming weaker. I winded easily and we were forced to take shorter walks. When that became too much, we sat on the porch instead. She asked all about the world. I asked all about her kids. We found peace in the opposite lives that we had lived. I no longer felt the doubts I had about the life I chose. Somehow, we seemed to complete each other.

Soon, my manuscript was complete. I sat my pen down and stared out across the backyard. The breeze gently pushed a long-abandoned swing back and forth. Somewhere, a bird trilled its mating song. I felt more relaxed than I had ever felt. I could live forever in the peace of that moment. The feeling lasted until I slipped into bed. I tossed and turned, thinking about what a terrible burden I was to my sister. The following morning, Sue Ellen found me sitting at the kitchen table. My bag was packed and at my side. She stood at the bottom of the stairs and frowned.

"I've been selfish … again," I said.

"Selfish?" She shook her head. "Everything is how it should be."

With the same look of determination that led her from that shack so many years ago, she grabbed my one bag and placed my clothes into the chest of drawers in the room that she called mine.

I never brought it up again.

A year and two months after leaving my apartment and driving halfway across the country, I awoke suddenly from a deep sleep. There was no pain, but a strange sensation washed over me. First, it was just a whisper, and then an urgent cry. I slipped from beneath my warm covers and ran down the hall. My bare feet slapped against the cool, wooden floor. Sue Ellen's room was at the very end. I eased open her door and slid beneath the covers on the side where her husband had slept. Sue Ellen felt different than I remembered, but then again, the same. She felt like home.

"Sue," I whispered.

"Hmmm?" she murmured before bolting up. "What is it? Are you okay?"

"I'm fine," I lied. "I just need you to do something for me."

"Anything," she whispered.

The moon was so bright that we didn't need the headlights. I rolled down the passenger window and closed my eyes as the night breeze blew across my face. The frogs and cicadas were loud with the sound of past summers and of summers I would never see.

Crunching rocks announced that we had arrived. I opened my eyes and nodded. At night and in the dark, the house looked just like it did when I left thirty-some years ago. Sue helped me out of the car, for I was so weak I could only walk a few steps before I had to stop. It took a long time to make our way across the yard and around the house.

I shuffled to the trunk of the old tree and nestled my finished manuscript between the gnarled roots. I smirked as I thought about the twenty-three-year-old girl who had left this place without so much as a backward glance. What would she think of me now?

I turned and smiled.

Sue Ellen had spread out a blanket under the branches. She patted the empty space beside her. I lay down feeling a slight pang of regret. But it only lasted a second.

As if she could read my mind, Sue Ellen reached for my hand and our fingers intertwined. She gave me a gentle squeeze. Little scraps of childhood memories fluttered silently in the wind as I smiled and closed my eyes.

Lynn's thoughts …

Sibling rivalry comes to mind when I read this story. Two sisters at odds with each other, competing and not even knowing. Who wins? In the end, neither.

The statement … *I lay down feeling a slight pang of regret …* hit home in many ways. Regret … how often do we regret doing something or saying something? But when it comes to time, there is simply no way of salvaging those hours … no way to retrieve them … to do it over again.

Our author captured the problem with time and how it has a habit of creeping up on us. The opening where we walk down memory lane of the old house. The visit to the store and being recognized. Her sister handing over a scrapbook filled with memories. And the tree that was decorated with strips of old dresses. All symbols of a time passed, a time that cannot be relived, a time that is gone.

What is refreshing about this story is how the sisters bond at the end. Their love and caring surround each other at a time when one of them is about to pass over. They stick together, and together, they sleep under those strips of old dresses … on the same land from where they began. Great ending …

- 114 -

Denise Israel

The porch ran the length of their ranch-style house. It was once open, but Iris had persuaded Reggie to enclose it. She hated bugs. Now, they sat outside, enjoying their coffee. Reggie wasn't handy working with wood and didn't want to impose on his friends for help. Iris said she'd help. All they had to do was tack up screening and plug any holes. If any bugs worked their way through, they'd keep plugging the holes. They were still young, and therefore, standing on ladders wasn't an issue. When it was finished, Iris didn't like the way it looked. Too sloppy, but the bugs stayed out.

"You want pie?" Iris asked.

"What kind?"

"What kind do you think?" she replied.

"Don't play guessing games. I just asked … what kind?"

"If I said *strawberry* what would you say?"

"I'd say, 'no thanks.'"

"That's why it's peach," she stated.

"Okay, I'll have some. Why didn't you say so?"

Iris thought about the nothings that were swirling in circles. She stood and fetched the pie and coffee. Then she sat in her rocking chair. Her hands fidgeted with the hem of her skirt that was coming loose. *Another thing to mend.* A black-winged bug was making its way into the corner of the netting. A dirt dauber's nest was on the outside of the screen, and one had entered, building a new home. She examined the netting from where she sat. There was fraying and areas that looked rusty and coming away from the frame.

"Reggie, do you see the dirt dauber?" She pointed.

Reggie followed her finger. "They're harmless. Leave it alone and it'll leave you alone."

"How many years ago did we put this netting up?"

"You have the answers," he replied. "How many?"

"Twenty-three. Nothing lasts that long without repairs, not even a refrigerator."

"You're hard to please. Always have been."

"You are just lazy and uninspired."

Iris stood and walked into the house. She hated their standoffs, but they were necessary to get the man off his duff.

Reggie sat on the porch, shaking his head. She always seemed to be able to blindside him. He never knew what she wanted. He could either stay on the porch and finish his pie or go inside and beg for forgiveness. Tonight, he was too tired. He turned on the radio and listened to the ballgame.

The next morning, he woke to no breakfast. Reggie puttered around the kitchen making his own. A note saying that Iris was off to the hair stylist and grocery store was just fine with him. Gathering his tennis gear, he headed to the courts.

I love Iris like I love tennis. She wears me out but keeps me in shape.

As Iris finished putting away the groceries, Reggie walked in through the back door. A wariness hung in the air. After putting his things away, he walked back for a glass of water. He nodded at Iris.

"Your hair looks nice," he said. "New style?"

She smiled. "No, but thanks."

"What do men know?" He grinned.

They laughed.

"Let's hire a contractor to redo the porch," he said, taking a sip of water.

"Really? What about the cost?"

"An anniversary gift," he replied. "To us."

"Sounds good." She wasn't too certain how good it was, for she couldn't shake the notion that anniversary gifts were supposed to be frivolous.

Their anniversary date Reggie could always keep straight. He bought a bouquet of irises and fancy Belgian chocolates. As much as they were a repeat, he knew she liked them. It was their twenty-seventh, that he was almost certain about. He did the math. In his opinion, she was an attractive fifty-one, and he was a good-looking, somewhat portly, sixty-one. Underneath the dye-job, he guessed her once-chestnut-colored hair was probably turning gray. His hair turned gray a while back and thinned to almost baldness. Iris thought he was still handsome, which satisfied him.

Iris' hobby was cooking fancy meals, and their anniversary dinner was something she had planned for many weeks. Several times she changed her mind before she decided. She wanted everything to be a piece of art, just like on the cooking shows. She baked two different pies and would choose which one depending on the mood of the evening.

Reggie never liked special occasions, and their anniversary was no exception. Iris set great value as to how it would play out, and he was never sure if the event lived up to her expectations or not. *Who could keep up with Iris and her dreams?*

Iris called from the kitchen. "Reggie?"

"Yes, my love."

"We'll be having hors d'oeuvres in thirty minutes."

"Can I do anything?"

"Get ready and you can mix our drinks."

Reggie knew the drill. He donned the shirt and pants she liked best. Combed the bit of hair that remained and practiced smiling in the mirror. "What are we drinking?" he yelled out.

"You know I love a good Cosmo," she yelled back. "You can make yourself a martini."

He stood at their tiny bar and pulled out the vermouth, gin, and vodka and called out, "Do we have cranberry juice and lime?

"No. I would have thought you'd pick 'em up?"

"I'll drive to the store. No problem. Be right back." He grabbed his orange sweater and ran out the back door. It was the wrong sweater. Iris hated orange and she had asked him to take it to Goodwill weeks ago. "She could have asked me to do this earlier. I make mistakes when I'm rushed."

From inside the kitchen, Iris muttered, "He had nothing to do but think about his bartending duties. That damned orange sweater!"

When he walked in with the cranberry juice and limes, Iris was sitting in the living room with her feet on the ottoman and her eyes closed. Smoked oysters on toasted rye were on the coffee table.

Iris was composing herself. She'd already taken two aspirins. She opened her eyes and gave him a smile. Reggie relaxed and began mixing the drinks.

"Here you are my dear," he said.

"Ahh, thank you. I needed this." She took a sip. It was excellent. "You still have your skills. One would think we had cocktails every night."

"One never forgets their moves."

They giggled.

After the drinks, they glided into the dining room. It was the nicest room in the house. Gracious in proportions, it was furnished with Iris' mother's antiques. With reluctance, she had agreed to hang Reggie's uncle's portrait that was painted in somber ochre oils. It gave most people pause when they came eye-to-eye with his penetrating gaze. She had set the table with their wedding China. Iris brought out a flank steak stuffed with mushrooms and garlic and whipped potatoes with broiled asparagus on the side.

Reggie's eyes were wide. "Smells divine." He poured the burgundy. "To us!"

Iris looked him in the eyes and smiled. "To us!"

Reggie studied her hands. They were looking old and gnarled. Glancing at his own, he paused, for his were also a little distorted. "You don't wear your rings anymore?"

"I was wondering when you would notice. I haven't worn rings for quite some time."

"Why? Arthritis?" He was the one with arthritis. His mother had been hobbled with it.

"I don't have arthritis."

"Then what is it?" he asked.

"I wasn't going to bring it up. But now that *you've* brought it up, I'll tell you before we have dessert."

They finished their meal with grunts of pleasure, and slowly finished off a bottle of wine. Reggie had a notion Iris wanted to talk about something he didn't want to talk about. Iris cleared the table, and they adjourned to their porch rocking chairs. Reggie felt unsteady on his feet as he made his way outside. Iris still had a spring in her step.

"Sit," she said. "The telling about the rings may take a while. Don't fall asleep or you won't get dessert. I'll get you a cup of coffee to give you some focus."

She had him where she wanted him. She fetched the coffee and settled into her rocker. "Do you remember the engagement ring?"

Reggie felt uncertain and wasn't sure if it was from being quizzed or if he had truly forgotten. "I'm not sure. You mean the one I gave you?"

"Do you remember what it looked like?"

Reggie thought for a few, long seconds and replied, "I thought it was beautiful. I was nervous with all the wedding plans. I'm sorry my mind's a blank."

"I can tell you why your mind's a blank. Our mothers chose the engagement ring. It was picked out by a committee a few days before our wedding. Any idea why?"

"No idea," Reggie stammered.

"Because *you* hadn't given me one, that's why." Iris let the concept sink in. "Remember?"

"No."

"Do you remember your mother saying to my mother, 'Does she have an engagement ring?' And my mother saying, 'No.' And your mother saying, 'The guests will expect to see one. I guess we'll have to buy it.' And then the four of us spent a day combing the town's jewelry stores. I finally picked the antique amethyst that was adequate. It had problems, mind you, that we didn't have time to fix. They were problems *you* said that *you* would fix and never did. Does any of this sound familiar?"

Reggie looked up at a cobweb and sighed. "Somewhat. What was the problem I needed to fix?"

"I wanted a flawless diamond instead of the amethyst."

"Ah, yes. I was working as a shipping clerk at the time. I remember now."

"I'll bring another cup of coffee," she said.

Reggie rubbed his neck and shifted in his rocker. His back was feeling stiff, but he dared not complain. Iris set the cups down and a little spilled onto the saucers. Reggie mopped his up with a napkin. She rocked with vigor and the floorboards creaked irritatingly.

"Then a few years later," she said, "you got your college degree in accounting and accepted the job with Watson and Stetson. That was a good-paying job."

Reggie looked up at the porch ceiling again and sighed. He watched as a spider crawled toward him. Not taking his eyes off it, he replied, "That job was stressful and you knew that. I was inexperienced and they expected a lot from me. I didn't have a moment to think about anything else."

"So I noticed. I guess that's why the amethyst ring went back inside its box."

Reggie took a gulp of his coffee, not daring to ask about dessert.

"I have to ask if you ever had a moment to think about anything else?"

"What do you mean?" he asked.

"We've been together a long time. Twenty-seven years to be exact. I need you to be truthful before we make it to thirty."

The spider moved above Reggie's head. He squirmed. If there were an insect he abhorred, it was a spider. He didn't know why. He had researched human fears. Apparently, humans had three primal anxieties ... heights, snakes, and spiders. Would he be able to sit under the spider and endure the spinning questions inside his head? *What if the spider dropped on me?*

"Get to the point," he stated. "I'm not sure I know what you're getting at."

"Do you know why I'm not wearing our wedding ring?"

"Of course not. It's a beautiful ring from a prominent jeweler. I made sure of that. You praised it when we were married."

"That's true. However, sometimes, *things* are not what they seem."

Reggie looked up again. The spider was now spinning a web just above his head. He wasn't wearing his glasses, so he couldn't tell what kind of spider it was. "Don't speak in riddles. I'm a simple man. Just state what's on your mind."

"I wish you were a simple man. However, once you were a devious man."

Reggie rocked and discovered that if he rocked forward, he could avoid the spider's downward path. The spider didn't seem interested in him, at least not for the moment. It was following its silk back and forth to the corner, almost in rhythm to his rocking.

"Don't you think the night is beautiful?" he asked. "The temperature is perfect. Do you want your sweater? You so often get a chill after the sun sets."

"I'm fine. Actually, I'm quite warm. Maybe too warm."

A brief silence before the cicadas chanted their rhythm. Reggie looked up and shuddered. The spider was carrying something wrapped in silk. It stopped at the partially spun web and stared down at him.

"How did you get our wedding bands?" she asked.

"I bought them."

"Is that true?" she asked.

"What are you saying?"

"You mean, you *paid* for them. Is that what you mean?"

"What else would I mean?"

"But *how* did you select them?"

Sweat ran from his forehead. He didn't believe that he had done anything wrong, but apparently he had. The spider was weaving the web in earnest, with the corpse of a black insect in the center. He fixed his eyes on it, but his sweat had fogged his glasses.

"Reggie … look at me. This entire time, you've been staring up at that ceiling. How rude."

Reggie's eyes met hers and all he could see were frightful black holes. He couldn't move. He tried to speak, but his throat felt dry.

"You need to confess," she said. "Were you the one who picked out our rings? Yes or no?"

Reggie sighed deeply. "No."

"Then who did?"

Reggie gazed at the ceiling. The spider was sucking on its prey, enjoying the kill.

"Who did?" she stated louder.

Reggie leaned his head back and replied, "Donna."

Iris stood and stared at him. "Donna, Donna, Donna. That whore! Donna, Donna, Donna. *She* chose our wedding rings? How could you be such a knave?" She sat down and crossed her arms.

Reggie wasn't sure what was so damning about what he had done so many years ago. She hadn't accused him of the worst yet. However, he still had to take a stand. His voice felt a little stronger and he spoke. "I didn't know anything about wedding rings. Donna was married twice. She had connections in Birmingham and offered to help."

"There's more to this story, isn't there?"

"I don't know what you mean?"

"Will the personal note written on the back of the receipt remind you of anything?" she asked.

The spider had finished his meal and was probably ready to pounce … on him. "Guessing games again? I have no idea what you are talking about."

"I'll read the note to refresh your memory. I found it with the older receipts. You have such a meticulous accountant's approach to saving such things. By the way, do you remember when she bought the rings?"

"No."

"The note is dated July 1st. Do you recollect the date we were married?"

Reggie took in a smaller breath. He knew this answer. "August 1st."

Iris laughed. "Lucky you remembered … or maybe not. Do you know where I was right before our wedding?"

Reggie felt a cold sweat coming on. The porch thermometer read seventy-five degrees, and the spider was hanging just above his left shoulder. He rocked back in the chair and imagined the creature landing on his arm. The two had come to a standstill with that *thing* hovering at just eye level. The spider's exoskeleton was brown and black with orange on its bulbous stomach. Large fangs were twitching, as if preparing for a strike. Reggie had seen a picture of this particular spider inside a book once but couldn't remember if it were poisonous or not.

He tried to keep an even tone when he replied, "I thought you were getting *things* ready for the wedding. There was talk about colors and candles and such."

"All that was already decided. I was tired and wanted to rest. I took a trip with my sister to Virginia Beach to tan in the sun. We were gone for about a week."

Reggie rocked farther back in his chair and hit the table. The coffee sloshed.

"Would you sit still, please?" she asked.

Reggie felt the critter land on his arm. It was too late to do anything. The pinch was hard and deep. He lowered his head and the sweat ran from his face. His shirt felt drenched. His chest pounded and his stomach clinched.

"Where was I?" she said. "Oh, yes. The note."

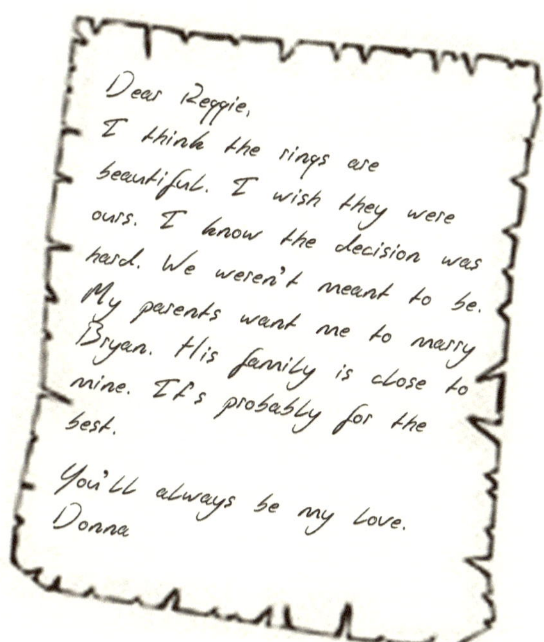

Reggie's face turned the color of grain, matching the gray-white hue of the spider's silk. The venom worked its way through his body, and his muscles refused to twitch. His rocker stood still.

"We can have dessert now," she stated. "I'll have strawberry pie."

Lynn's thoughts …

Would this story fall under resentment … retaliation … or jealousy? Any of these emotions can be destructive – to either party. Usually it starts with jealousy before moving to resentment and then to retaliation.

Relationships – one of the most difficult things to define. How do we describe our interactions? Love … acceptance … tolerance? Are these three words exclusive or inclusive?

The use of a spider's venom to demonstrate the pain of a dysfunctional marriage was quite interesting. But it worked. The wife harboring her jealousy since before the marriage could be considered the spider, and the bite was when she finally received her revenge. The marriage could be represented by the web that is weaved throughout the years. The man is caught in his own web of deceit, and the woman understands as she continuously patches the holes. That is, until they cannot take any more patching and she eats her mate. Well, not literally, but close.

It's interesting how Reggie knows that the bite is coming but does nothing to prevent it. In some respect, it's as if he deserves the punishment, for he has already stood trial. Reggie said he was a simple man. His wife corrected him, however, saying that he was a devious man.

Was he devious by being naïve or was there more? I guess we'll never know, will we?

How About Some Pie

Kathleen Fine

"Gina Fortier? Your license, ma'am." The lady behind the glass slid the small plastic card under the partition.

Gina let out a long sigh as she read the information next to her photo. "New York State. Gina Fortier. Sex: F. Eyes: BL. HT: 6-02." She wiped away a tear as she reread that one line. "Gina Fortier. Sex: F."

For the last fourteen years, her ID had said something different. *She* was something different. When she first walked into this DMV office at the age of sixteen, *she* was a young *he*. A confused boy, just wanting his license so he could leave Buffalo and live in the city. But now, here *she* was, and although still in Buffalo, Gina was a grown, mature woman.

"Thank you," Gina said as she held the treasure near her heart. Placing the card in her wallet, she wasn't sure if that woman had just given her that *judgmental* look or not. Didn't matter anyway. People could stare all they wanted, for Gina was, according to the State of New York, a woman. And she had a new name and driver's license to prove it.

As she walked toward the exit, her phone buzzed from her clutch. She sighed, remembering that it was her dad's sixty-ish birthday and tonight was the dinner. Her mom was probably calling to remind her.

"Brian?"

Her mother's voice rang through her ear before she could say *hello*. Gina grimaced at the name. No one had called her Brian in over ten years. Why wouldn't her mom understand?

"Gina … Mom!" Gina stated firmly. "It's Gina!" She refused to be treated this way by her own mother.

"Brian, Gina, whatever you call yourself. Are you meeting us at Applebee's for Dad's birthday? You can't be late, you know, and you're always late." Her mother's yorkie yapped in the background.

"Yes, Mom," Gina replied. "You reminded me yesterday. And the day before that. And the day before that. I'll be there." Gina felt frustrated as her phone beeped. "I have a call I have to take. See you soon. Love you." Gina clicked over to her friend, Virginia. "This is Gina," she said formally, as if answering a business call.

"Is that my strong queen?" a familiar voice boomed.

"You like that I went with Fortier? It's not too much?" Gina asked as she pressed unlock on her fob and slid into her silver Lincoln Nautilus.

"No, I *love* that you chose a last name with meaning. You are the strongest woman I know. Why wouldn't you go with Fortier? Besides, what kind of a name was Whitehead? When I first met you and you told me your last name, all I thought about was a big pimple."

Gina laughed and turned her car onto Swan Street.

"Can we celebrate tonight?" Virginia asked. "Ladies' night and somewhere nice?"

"I can't," Gina said. "It's my dad's sixty-ish birthday. I'm headed to Applebee's now. There probably aren't enough skinny margaritas in that place to get me through this dinner."

"Oh, girl!" Virginia screeched. "You're going right now? The only people there are gonna be you and some geriatric customers. It's still daylight."

"I know, but my parents won't drive past dark," Gina said as she stopped for a red light. She checked her lipstick in the rear-view mirror.

"Then let's go for drinks after?" Virginia offered. "Nine o'clock? Boxwood?"

Boxwood was their *go-to* spot for a guaranteed good time. Gina smiled, making sure that she didn't have lipstick on her teeth.

"See you then," Gina said with a grin. Knowing that she would be meeting Virginia later would help her get through her family's dinner.

"See you then, Miss Queen." Virginia hung up.

As she pulled into the parking lot, she could see that her parents were already there with her younger sister, Rosemary. Rosemary still lived with their parents, even though she'd just celebrated her twenty-third birthday and was more than capable of living on her own. Gina couldn't imagine living with her parents. She had moved out as soon as she turned eighteen … although her dad told everyone that *he* kicked *her* out. However, she knew the truth. She left of her own free will.

"Happy birthday, Dad," Gina said as she crossed the parking lot. She handed him a present and smiled.

The heavyset man with a permanent growl glared at her as if she were intruding on their private evening. "Hello, Brian." He hesitantly accepted the present. His eyes trailed from her head down to her toes. "You look … *interesting* … as always. Hope we don't see anyone we know." He handed the present to her mother and aimed for the entrance. Her mom smiled before following her father's lead.

"New highlights?" Rosemary asked as she walked next to Gina.

Gina touched her hair, almost forgetting that she had bleached it to a summer blonde. "Yeah, felt I needed something a little lighter." Gina held the door for Rosemary.

"Looks nice," Rosemary replied as she stepped inside.

As she followed her family to the table, Gina could sense that all eyes were focused on her. People were whispering, giving her the once over. Or maybe they weren't looking at her at all. Maybe it was just her imagination. It usually was her imagination. She sat next to Rosemary and faced her dad.

"So, Dad," Gina said. "Did you do anything special for your birthday?" She opened the menu and scanned through the drinks. Maybe she would order a vodka soda instead of a margarita. Or maybe red wine.

"Fixed the lawn mower," he replied. "That thing's been acting up." He opened his napkin and placed it on his lap.

"That's great," Gina said, trying to be respectful.

A young waitress approached who appeared to be younger than Rosemary. "Welcome to Applebee's. My name's Amanda and I'll be serving you today. Can I bring some drinks while you look over the menu?" She pulled a pad of paper and pen from her apron.

"Budweiser for the birthday boy," her dad said before anyone could answer.

"Happy birthday, sir," Amanda said, scribbling down his order.

"I'll have a strawberry daquiri with extra whipped cream," her mom said with a sneer. "It's a special occasion so I'll *indulge* myself."

"I'll have a rum and coke," Rosemary said.

"Vodka soda," Gina stated. She needed some alcohol and quick.

"Okay, so that's a Budweiser, strawberry daquiri, rum and coke, and vodka soda?" Amanda repeated. "Sorry, but I have to ask anyone who looks under the age of thirty for their IDs." She looked directly at Gina and Rosemary.

Gina couldn't tell if this was the truth, or if Amanda, their waitress, was snooping. Perhaps she wanted to investigate. As she pulled out her ID, a sensation of pride and shame hit.

Amanda read over Rosemary's ID and nodded. She grabbed Gina's and inspected it. She stared at Gina, looked at the ID, and inspected Gina again.

"Is there a problem?" Gina asked, adjusting herself on her seat. "I'm clearly older than my sister, and you gave hers back right away."

"No," Amanda replied. "No problem." She handed the ID back. "Sorry about that, Ms. Fortier."

Feeling flushed, Gina shoved her ID inside her wallet, wishing she had said *no* to the invitation for dinner. She already had to spend time with them on Thanksgiving and Christmas. *Why do I always do this to myself? Why do I bother spending time with them when I feel not one ounce of confidence or happiness in their presence?*

"Did she say Fortier?" her mother asked. She looked at Gina with a gaze of confusion.

How can I feel so empowered and strong one moment, and the next feel only two feet tall? "She did," Gina replied, sitting up a little straighter.

"Why would she say that, Brian?" her dad asked, pulling a toothpick from his pocket and placing it in his mouth.

"Because that's my last name now," Gina said. "And my first name is Gina. Not Brian. I had it changed legally. Therefore, I'd appreciate it if you'd remember to call me by my *correct* name."

"You changed it legally?" her mother asked. "What if you decide to go back to Brian Whitehead?"

Amanda stepped up with a tray of drinks.

"I've never *been* Brian Whitehead," Gina said. "I need to use the restroom." She locked eyes with the waitress and smiled. The bathroom was across from the bar. As she passed a table of men, they eyed her.

Are they liking what they see? Why should she care? She'd never date a man who ate in an Applebee's anyway. She opened the door to the lady's room as a woman with short, blonde hair was leaving.

"Excuse me," Gina said, holding the door open for the woman.

The woman, who was in her mid-to-late-fifties, was about a foot shorter than Gina. She glanced up and her eyes widened. "Excuse me?" She frowned before scurrying away.

Did I frighten her?

For the most part, Gina looked like a woman ... her breasts, her clothes, her hair. Even the hormones made her voice a little more feminine. But it was her height and her feet. No amount of money in the world would ever change those. It would always be more difficult for her to blend in. All she wanted was to blend in.

As she finished in the bathroom, Gina applied more mascara to her faux eyelashes. She always made sure not to buy lashes that were too long. Afterall, she wasn't trying to look like a *drag* queen. She wasn't a *drag* queen. She *was* a woman. A woman whose name meant *strong queen.* Gina zipped her purse and as she aimed for the door, a large man wearing a leather Harley jacket walked in. His eyes were huge and wild-looking.

"I think you have the wrong bathroom, sir," Gina said, taking a step back. "This is the *ladies* room."

The man stared at Gina and a rage burned from behind his eyes.

Gina's knees felt weak.

"No, I think *you* have the wrong bathroom, SIR!" He said as he stepped closer. "You nearly scared the life out of my wife walking in here, you circus freak!" He grabbed at her.

Gina screamed and fumbled through her purse looking for her ID.

"What do you got under there, huh?" The man grabbed at her dress and lifted it up. "You like to pretend to be a woman just so you can steal a peek in the bathroom, you sick pervert?"

Gina stumbled backward as the man slapped her hard across her face. Her tears fell and blood trickled down her cheek.

"Stop it!" she screamed, scrambling around in her purse. "I'm a woman. My name's Gina Fortier. I'm a woman. I have a license to prove it." Her voice deepened from her panic, sounding more masculine. Hearing her voice so deep was almost worse than the pain running through her cheek. She gave up looking for the ID and kneed the man in the groin.

He dropped to the floor. She pushed the door open and darted into the restaurant. All eyes were definitely on her this time. *Why do all eyes always have to be on me? What must I look like to them?* Her dress was hiked up. She had tears streaming down her face. She had blood on her cheeks. She locked eyes with her parents from across the restaurant. They looked embarrassed. She ran toward the exit and darted for her car. *Why did I come here?* She pulled out of the parking lot and sped down 190 toward the rest stop, wiping mascara-filled tears from her eyes. Pulling into the closest spot, she turned off her car.

She grabbed a tissue from the compartment and dabbed at the blood on her lip. She opened her clutch and pulled out her wallet. She looked at her license and read …

New York State

Gina Fortier

Sex: F

She closed her eyes and leaned back. "I am a woman. My name is Gina Fortier. I'm a woman. I have a license to prove it." She whispered the words as she stared at her treasure. She started the car and aimed it toward Virginia's house, clutching the ID tightly in her fist.

Lynn's thoughts …

Changing one's gender is an interesting concept. Not sure if I would want to switch – sounds quite painful in more ways than one. I've studied gender dysphoria, and therefore, hold sympathy for those afflicted. However, I must ask whether changing one's gender is a byproduct of not feeling accepted by those we consider as being *normal*? Then again, what *is* normal?

If everyone were accepted for who or what they were, no matter how odd or weird or different or normal, then would there be a rush to undergo such a drastic procedure?

Then again … body alteration is nothing new. Various tribes throughout the ages have worked diligently to change their looks – skull elongation, neck stretching, severe piercings, tattooing by raising the skin, the list goes on and on.

I wonder how many years will pass before we can change a person's chromosomes. Our bodies switch out our cells every seven to ten years. Therefore, if we could somehow notify the new cells to change … hmmm. What a concept. Then again, men can be men with no Y chromosome. And a woman can be a woman with a Y chromosome. Therefore, does it really matter? Not sure.

It will be interesting to look back in about fifty years and review everything that happened. We just need to be careful. If we evolve too far, we may end up not being able to reproduce. Perhaps that would solve the problem. After all, if there were no humans, then there would be no issues of feeling left out, would there?

Frank Shima

Sam's cowlick refused to stay put.

Behave!

That was what his mom always said. Sam never behaved or couldn't, just like his cowlick. Not like his brother – his *good* little brother. There wasn't a hair out of place on that kid's head.

Timmy received all the praise in the family. Even though he was three years older, Sam never received any praise. Timmy was a seven-year-old angel who never did anything wrong. At least, not that his mother ever noticed.

Sam glanced into the bathroom mirror and frowned at his freckled face and the ears that stuck out like weather vanes checking for the direction of his mother's wind. He licked his hand and patted down the curl. It stayed in place.

"Sam!" his mother yelled. "Your dinner's getting cold. How long does it take to wash your hands?"

"Be right down." Sam glanced at the mirror again and noticed that the cowlick was now out of place. He shrugged and ran down the stairs, clinging to the banisters as he took two steps at a time.

Timmy was already at the table shoveling a spoonful of potatoes into his mouth.

His mom tapped her foot with her hands on her hips and glared at him. "Quit dawdling. Your brother is waiting for you. You know he won't eat until you're at the table."

Sam ran to his chair and sat down. His leg clipped the side of the table and his glass of milk fell over.

"Sam!" his mother yelled out. "Can't you be more careful?"

He tried to shrink his ears so he wouldn't hear what was coming next.

"Just wait until your father gets home."

Those were not the words he was expecting. His mom always threatened him with that empty threat. But he was usually asleep when his dad returned, and he was gone before his father woke up.

"Why can't you be more like your father?" she asked.

That was it. Those were the words.

If I saw him once in a while, then maybe I could. That was what he wanted to say. But he didn't. Sam didn't know his father, not really. Not the way Bobby next door knew his dad.

Sometimes, Sam wished he was Timmy. Timmy looked like a younger version of his dad. He didn't own an annoying cowlick, and his ears were tiny, almost non-existent. A little piece of Sam also existed in his mom. The eyes. Those cold, accusatory, and soul-piercing eyes. Sam wondered where he actually fit inside this perfect family, since he didn't look like either of his parents. Maybe he was adopted, and his true birth parents would someday knock on the front door and whisk him away. Not that anyone would care or notice.

Sam's mom, with great drama, sponged up the spilled milk. Preaching about wasting food and the starving children in Indiana, Sam laughed. He knew that she meant India. He wanted to correct her but knew better. When she had finished wiping up the spill, Sam half-expected her to wring the milk back into his glass. She didn't.

And Timmy, who couldn't eat a meal without Sam's presence, had already finished and left the table.

Sam sat alone, which was probably supposed to be a punishment from his mother. His mashed potatoes were cold. He glanced into the living room where Timmy was using the coffee table as a racetrack and scratching the surface with his tiny racecars.

The screen door slammed, and he glanced up at his father who placed his battered lunch box on the counter. He gave Sam a quizzical look. "What are you doing eating alone? Or should I say *not eating*?"

"Cold potatoes." Sam lifted his fork and shrugged.

"He should have eaten them when they were warm," his mother stated. "He's being punished. You need to talk to him about his attitude."

"What'd he do wrong now?"

"Spilled his milk."

"And?"

"And what?" she screamed.

"He must have done something. Did he rob a bank? All kids spill milk."

She grabbed Sam's plate and scraped the potatoes into the garbage. "So easy for you to say, isn't it? You're not here all day like I am. You don't know. How could you?"

His dad was about to say something but hesitated.

"Can I go outside?" Sam asked.

"Don't interrupt, Sam. Can't you see that your father and I are talking?"

"Go outside," his dad said. "Hang around. We'll go to McDonald's later."

"I don't think he should be rewarded …" his mother said as he ran out the back door.

The screen slammed.

What reward? He hated McDonald's but at least he would be with his father. For some reason, he was good when he was with him.

Sam sat on the cool cement steps and waited. His huge ears could pick up parts of the argument that continued on inside the kitchen. The rest, he simply chose to ignore. Instead, he thought of pleasant things that could never happen. Of a life where a family lived in peace and harmony. Of a life where he could spend more time with his father. Of a life where he could be around his little brother a lot less. Of a life where his mom loved him, well, maybe just liked.

The sudden silence interrupted his thoughts. He turned and squinted to see better through the screen door. His parents were kissing again. They seemed to do that a lot these days. His mom broke away and smiled at his father. A tender, loving, and beautiful smile. If only he were more like his dad, then maybe his mother wouldn't hate him so much.

Sam's dad, true to his promise, took him to McDonald's. With his father's arm draped over his shoulder, they walked to the pickup truck. As they pulled out of the yard, Sam glanced back to see his mother standing at the back door, and her smile slowly transformed into an ugly scowl.

Sam sat in the visitor's chair that bumped up to the warden's oak desk. The office, in stark contrast to the rest of the prison, was beautifully decorated with brightly painted walls and ornate paintings in wooden frames.

The trip to McDonald's was interrupted when his dad remembered something he had forgotten at work. It must have been important because he didn't drop Sam off at home. Sam had never been to his dad's office. In fact, he didn't even know where his father worked … especially in a prison.

As he waited, he watched the second hand on the clock click and tried to imagine what his father's job was. It had to be important if the warden needed to see him.

The door to the office opened, and a haggard-looking man with stringy, gray hair stood in the doorway. He was wearing a prison uniform with the numbers 537199 over the front pocket. He limped into the office, and Sam noticed that his pant legs were frayed at the ends. Number 537199 emptied the wastebasket into the cart and stared at Sam.

"What you doin' in here, boy?"

"Waiting for my dad."

"Your dad? Your dad's getten out today?"

"No. My dad went somewhere with the warden."

Number 537199 shook his head and let out an eerie laugh. It was a sound that gave Sam the creeps.

"So that's your father, boy?" Number 537199 asked. "Ain't that something? Didn't think a man like that could have a kid. Not with what he does for a livin'."

Sam held his breath for a second and watched as the man wiped down the desk. "What does my dad do here?"

Number 537199 turned and smiled. "Don't you know, boy? Why, he's the executioner."

"Executioner?"

"Yep, he puts us to sleep forever in that death chamber of his." Number 537199 took a step closer to Sam.

Sam sunk deeper into his chair.

"No need to be afraid of me, son. My name's Gus." Gus took another step and reached out a hand.

"Stay away!" Sam jumped up and ran behind the warden's desk.

Gus stepped up and laughed again. "I ain't gonna hurt you nun."

"Gus!" the warden stated. "Stop it right there."

"I wasn't doin' nutten, Warden."

"Do you want your days as a trustee to end?" the warden asked.

Gus backed away and shook his head. He glanced over at Sam and winked before ambling out of the office.

"Sorry about that," the warden said. "Gus is okay. As long as he's not around little boys."

The branch groaned as Sam ferociously soared back and forth on the old, wooden swing. He allowed his mind to wander through the dark shadows that seemed to close in on him. He thought about his father pulling the switch. He thought about how the body would quiver and then smoke before sitting limp. He couldn't get the pictures out of his mind. The images kept playing over and over again. Maybe the centripetal force of the swing would push away his thoughts.

His father was kind and gentle. If anyone in the family were capable of doing that job, it would be his mother, but not his father. She dealt out Sam's punishments like his teachers handed out homework. Sam could sense a hint of pleasure in his mother's eyes when she scolded him. The same eyes that were blind to any flaws of his little brother.

"Sam," his mother yelled. "Get in here!"

Now what? He kept swinging, hoping whatever it was would go away.

"I said get in here!" she screamed.

Somehow, Sam knew it would not go away. He slowed to a stop and ran into the kitchen.

"You took your sweet time," his mother stated.

Her face was red, and she glared at him with her eyes on fire and her hands plastered to her hips. She grabbed him by the arm and dragged him into the living room.

"What do you know about these scratches on the coffee table?"

Sam knew everything about them. But he had been through this many times before. He tried the silent approach.

"I asked you a question! What do you know about this?"

"Nothing," he answered.

"Nothing! How can you say that?"

Silence didn't work and neither did lying. So, he decided to go with the truth. "Timmy did it with his cars."

"How can you blame your little brother? He's been in his room all day. It's bad enough you do these things, but to lay it on Timmy? You can stay in your room for the rest of the day. No supper. And if you have any idea of manipulating your father into taking you to McDonald's again, you can just forget it. I don't know why you can't be more like your father."

The next day began harmlessly enough. Sam ate the same, boring breakfast followed by working through his chores while Timmy played in the yard. Sam was putting the breakfast dishes away when his mother rushed into the kitchen.

"Sam, get in the car. You know we're supposed to be at your dad's Halloween party."

This was the first Sam had heard of it.

"I've got to get your brother ready. Get in the car. I don't want to have to wait for you."

Sam sat in the car, waiting for his mother.

"What are we going to do at Daddy's work?" Timmy asked.

"We're going to a party. Doesn't that sound like fun?"

Sam couldn't understand how that would be fun for anyone.

When they arrived at the prison, the security guard checked his mother's identification. The huge, heavy gates opened, and she drove into the parking lot. They walked past dozens of locked doors and eventually were ushered into the cafeteria that was decorated with black-and-orange balloons and streamers, and with skeletons taped to the walls. The prisoners sat on one side of the room with grim faces.

Sam, Timmy, and his mother joined his father and other families on the other side. No one there was smiling, either. The children were all dressed in Halloween costumes. But not Sam. It was Sam's punishment for scratching the coffee table.

The warden finished his short speech, and a round of applause echoed through the room. The families were given a tour of the prison, and Sam was bored after a few minutes of looking into cell after cell where each was identical to the other. Finally, they walked into a gymnasium.

"Can I play, Mom?" Timmy asked.

"No, honey. I'm sorry."

Then they entered the huge room with an indoor swimming pool.

"Can I go swimming, Mom?" Timmy asked.

"No, honey. I'm sorry."

The last stop was the execution chamber which held the electric chair. The warden explained how an inmate would be strapped in and demonstrated pulling the switch.

"How disgusting," one mother said.

"Was that really necessary?" another asked.

"Lighten up," Sam's mother responded. "It's Halloween!"

They sat down to lunch, and Sam was starving. He was about to take his first bite when Timmy spilled his cranberry juice.

"Sam!" his mother yelled out. "Can't you be more careful?"

Sam knew better than to say anything. Although his brother was always in the wrong, Sam was the one to answer for it.

"Take your brother to the men's room and clean him up."

"They've been gone a long time," Sam's dad said.

"You know how Sam likes to dawdle," his mother replied.

"They were supposed to be right back."

"Sam kept asking to go the gym or swimming," his mother stated. "He better not have taken Timmy there."

Several guards gathered around the warden, and their voices echoed through the room. As they headed toward different doors, Sam's dad stopped one as he passed.

"What's going on?"

"Gus is missing," the guard whispered. "Probably nothing. Could be he's back in his cell."

"Gus is missing?" Sam's dad repeated. "We better find the boys."

Sam's dad followed the guard while his mother checked the nearest men's room. The place held a strong odor of stale urine. No boys. She checked the swimming pool. Timmy was not floating lifeless on the water as she had feared. She opened the door to the gymnasium. Empty. She asked each guard she met along the way if they had seen her two boys. However, no one had seen them.

Perhaps Sam had locked them in a cell. It would be just like something Sam would do. Her Timmy would be so frightened. She walked down another hall and glanced through the window of the execution chamber. A smiling Sam stood tall next to the electric chair.

"Oh my God, Sam! What have you done?"

"Timmy needed to be punished, Mom," Sam said, smiling.

His mother ran to the lifeless body of her precious Timmy who was slumped over the armrest. She rubbed her nose from the odor of burnt hair and flesh.

"Sam, why?" she cried out.

"Now, I'm just like Daddy."

Lynn's thoughts …

The eldest child … for some reason, many first borns believe they exist under stricter rules. Not sure if this is one hundred percent correct, although it definitely seems that way. Parents tend to expect their eldest to be good role models for the littler ones. Does that make the eldest resentful? Maybe.

Then again, how many of the older ones always feel as if they are in charge? My siblings did. And us younger ones were usually considered a nuisance, a negative to deal with. Hey, I only stole my sister's makeup once. I needed it for my doll!

If a child reflects what they see in their parents, then what can this story tell us?

The author captures the moment at this point …

Sam could sense a hint of pleasure in his mother's eyes when she scolded him.

Children have a way of sensing certain things in adults. It's a gift that is eventually lost as we age. It is similar to enjoying the aroma of freshly cut grass. The feel of an early spring morning. Or the best … playing after dark on a warm fall evening. As an adult, we no longer find pleasure in the little things. But our children do. And with the ability to absorb the simple, they also notice things. Lots of things. And they seek out praise.

Although this story took the situation to the extreme, the author made an excellent point and validated the importance of making all our children feel loved, cherished, valued, and wanted.

Just Like Daddy

Mouth Sewn Shut

Mary Fox

Mother hunched so deeply over the chest of drawers that her head almost disappeared. She seemed to be studying the aging, white coffee rings etched into the wooden surface. Her fingers were working a skein of Blu-Tack and kneading it into a gloopy mess. The darkening afternoon felt gloomy, and I hated this room, my sister's room.

"Did you write anything down?"

"I dreamt I was naked," I replied. "And Pauline Jackson was chasing me with a knitting needle."

"Anything about Dolores?" Mother twisted the tack tighter around her long fingers.

"I don't dream about Dolores. Too much –"

"There must be something in that head of yours. What did you hear? Where were they? You must have seen something."

Feeling irritated, I sighed. How many times will Mother ask? I said, over and over again, that my memories were hazy. Everything happened months ago. I only remembered dark strangers.

It was an evening toward the end of fall. We were entering that dead zone just before Christmas. I remembered that Halloween decorations were still flapping in the breeze on one of the houses at the edge of Streatham Common. My sister had picked me up from school, as our mother was taking an extra night shift at the hospital. We walked back to our house along a deserted path through the rookery. Although autumn had stripped the trees weeks ago, the roses were still in full bloom. Their glow against the blackness of the foliage seemed odd to me. Almost a premonition. The coarse cawing of the rooks roosting in the branches and the woody fragrance of bonfires filled the air and masked the darkening shapes that moved between the bushes.

It was the scuffling and screaming that filled me with a dread more painful than if I had been ripped in half. Therefore, I had to hide. It was between the holly bushes and where the branches were poking against my skin that I felt like I was being branded. A branding that would forever scar my thoughts and life. My fingers filled my ears as I hummed and hummed away the roaring evil that played out only a few feet away.

My teddy, Soft Mary, pressed against my thigh, reminding me that I was real and that everything else was real too. Forever I hid between those searing branches. When the world quieted, Dolores was gone. Except for her one patent leather shoe. I always wondered why they had taken my sister and left her shoe. Wouldn't she need her shoe? A million times, I counted on my fingers the possible reasons as to why and never once came up with an answer.

Dolores was older than me. A lot older. Six years, in fact. Her hair was the color of the beech trees in autumn. My hair was different, blonde and frizzy. Dolores had friends, lots of friends. I only had my teddy, Soft Mary. Dolores was tall and walked with her head held high, touching the clouds, where I was short and rooted into the earth like a sleeping mushroom. Perhaps that was why she wouldn't need her shoe. Dolores was thin and spry, whereas I was heavier and stuck to the ground. Immoveable. I was mulling over those facts one day when I spotted blood on her shoe. Her shoes were always brighter and shinier than mine. Something I always admired.

People had scurried about yelling and carrying torches. An older man asked if I was alright. Of course, I said yes. Someone called out my name. It was our local postman, Mr. Briars. His eyes were wide and bloodshot.

They took my sister. They took Dolores.

There was a swift shift of expression in Mr. Briars' eyes as if it had registered what he had said to me and how I had answered. More people arrived. I shivered as they shouted out Dolores' name. I didn't know the men who had pulled her out from under the bushes and dragged her away. So, I dropped Soft Mary instead, and she stared into the clouds. Her eyes were wide and blank and emotionless.

What's happening?

Dolores was here, walking next to me. Now she was gone. Would Soft Mary leave me too? Their eyes were the same in the end, wide open and blank.

For some reason, Mother wanted to talk about that day. Every hour, she asked more and more questions.

"It was windy," I said. "Pumpkins were still outside the house on Streatham Common."

"For Christ's sake, Martha. You can remember every bloody detail about the pumpkins. The way the mouth was lop-sided, and the seeds were puking out of it. But you can't remember a single thing about those … those men?" Her voice cracked.

An icy blade slid under my heart. I wanted to stuff my fingers into my ears again. Instead, I wiped away a tear. "I've tried. I really have." Another tear fell but I left it alone. "It was the puking pumpkin that made me laugh."

"Laugh? Jesus, Martha. Do you know how I've suffered? Normal children would have remembered something. Run for help or scream out. You do realize that your sister –"

My sister what? The words hung in the air like a swinging corpse. My sister what? She was smarter – prettier – and of course, braver. I already knew that.

"I told you to write things in the notebook. As soon as you wake up in the morning write it down. You're the only witness. The only one that was there. The nice policeman who came here and talked to you. He said to write things down, didn't he? So, write something. Anything."

Her fists hit the chest with such force that a poster of Marc Bolan floated free from its moorings. His black, kohl-rimmed eyes flashed from under his mane of shiny curls.

She stopped at the door but didn't turn. "There's another one here to speak to you. Another policeman." With a tighter tone, she added, "Please … tell him what you know."

The last policeman wasn't all that nice. His long nose hair and broken cheek veins looked as if he belonged someplace else. The new one was much younger, and his hair was a bright red. He peered around the door before rapping on it twice.

"Knock, knock," he whispered.

I nodded.

He took off his helmet and ruffled his thinning thatch of strawberry blonde. "May I ask a few more questions, Miss Nicholls?" He spoke very soft and slow.

"You haven't asked any yet."

He coughed a few times. "What do you remember?"

"Not much."

He pulled out his notepad and glanced down the page. "You had said there were two shadows in the bushes? Correct?"

I nodded. "I was counting the white roses. Roses are not supposed to bloom in the colder air."

"Were they tall shadows or short and fat ones?" he asked.

"I don't know."

"What did you hear when you saw the shadows?" he asked.

"The rooks. They were on the higher branches."

"You said you heard screaming?" The policeman's voice tightened.

"You asked what I heard when I first saw the shadows." I stared at him and wondered if he liked his red hair. Would I want red hair? No, I wanted hair like my sister's, dark and sleek and shiny.

"Let's try something different. How do you feel about losing your sister?"

I squinted and allowed the light to filter through. How does one feel after losing a sister? Sad? Lonely? What a sick question. "Like someone cut me open and took out my stuff. Then they put it back inside but backwards."

The policeman widened his gaze. "A vivid description."

"You asked."

"Did you love your sister?"

"What?"

"Did you love her?"

"Of course."

"Yet you did nothing to save her," he said, writing something on his paper.

I glared at him. My heart pounded and my stomach tightened. It felt as if he were punching me in my gut. I took in a deeper breath and replied, "I wasn't there."

"But you were found hiding in the bushes."

"My mind takes me places when I'm afraid."

"Convenient," he muttered.

I squinted at him again, and he licked the end of his pencil. As he wrote, he frowned.

"Mother says everything's been shot to shit now that Dolores is gone."

"And you?" he whispered. "What do you think?"

"Me?"

"Yes, you. How do you feel?" He adjusted the helmet that he held under his arm.

"I just want her to come home."

He sighed and I was reminded of the ugly one. That all too familiar mixture of anger and confusion filled me with dread. It was the truth. Why couldn't anyone understand? I had simply not been there.

The policeman stopped and spoke to Mother before leaving. He kept shaking his head, and Mother kept her eyes locked on her shoes.

I felt puzzled. Last night, I had to make my own supper. Beans and fish fingers, my favorite. I tried to open the can, but the old opener just left puncture marks around the edges. Now, my thoughts were swimming around inside that tin and becoming lost between the jagged edges. How was I to connect my memories to the rest of the world if the lines were so messy and irregular? It was impossible to single them out, just like last night when I couldn't get the beans out of that stupid can.

Eventually and with a lot of hard work, I pulled the lid free. My hand slipped and the jagged edge sliced through my skin. I stared at the crimson beads that popped up. I didn't cry. Not at first. Instead, I was relieved that the beans were liberated. When my blood dripped down my hand, I screamed. Mother dragged me to the sink and held my bleeding finger under the tap.

Life was a struggle. Probably because I was such a bad person. I never belonged in this world. Would be nice to be on my own. Walking to school alone and playing with the dogs along the way was perfect but always made me late for class. It was all because of those beans. How many beans were in that can, and how many of those thoughts filled my head?

Every day, I had to listen to my mother. Why do you nap during the day? Where do you go when you disappear for hours? Mother was always interrogating me. But Dolores was the one who protected me.

"Don't worry, Mum. She's just being Martha."

I was never sure what people wanted from me. Therefore, I spent time guessing, or pretending, or trying to fit in. Not because I wanted to but because that was what was expected of me. Now, it was just me and Mother. We simply tolerated each other. Being civil because we shared the same kitchen. Mother was right about one thing – everything was shot to shit after Dolores left.

"What did I do wrong?" I glanced over at Soft Mary and frowned. "It's cuz I'm not Dolores. Isn't it?"

If only I could be more like my sister. Maybe look or act like her. Then everything would be okay again.

The room was just as Dolores had left it. The same sheets and they had the same smell. A bottle of Oil of Olay, a lipstick, black mascara with the lettering worn off the side, a pendant with two halves of a broken heart, Paddington bear that Phil gave her two Christmases ago, and an old Jackie magazine.

A large hat box with a hinge was sticking out from under her bed. It was covered in pastel flower decoupage, and the name DOLORES was scrawled across it in my sister's distinctive and spidery handwriting. I opened it carefully. A ticket from the Wimbledon F.C. versus Celebrity Eleven football match sat atop a photo of Dolores and me from a Christmas party. Under that was a lock of her hair inside a plastic Jiffy bag. I had cut it off while she slept. I laughed. A few cheap rings that I had found in an old dressing table and had given to her. A pink baby shoe from the Clarkes down the street with a little bear on it. And a brown paper envelope with one of Dolores' school reports in it.

At the bottom was that shoe. The black patent pump that I saved from the rookery last October. When I went back to rescue Soft Mary, I had found the bloody shoe. It was hidden under some dried leaves. Specks of black mud were on the heel with rust-colored patches inside. My heart pounded. I had seen this shoe many times since I found it. The red and brown patches were not rust or mud. No, they were Dolores' dried blood. I had brought it home and hid it from Mother. It was my secret and private piece of Dolores and all I had left. The police had found Dolores' clothes, torn and bloody, in the park. Her other shoe was left hanging from a bush in the rose garden.

Picking up that shoe, I studied it. Was Marc Bolan watching me? Slowly and cautiously, I licked the leather until a tiny speck of my sister's blood rested on my tongue. I closed my eyes and remained there for a few, long moments. The afternoon sun felt warm against my face. The blood dissolved, and the iron twang had all but disappeared.

I stood in front of the long, beveled mirror that was next to Dolores' bed. The room had been decorated like this for as long as I could remember. How many times had I watched Dolores admire herself in this mirror? Smoothing her hair, de-clogging her mascara, or pressing her full red lips into a tissue? A couple of evenings before she left, Dolores had offered to help me with my makeup. It frightened me at first.

"You could be popular if you only tried," Dolores had said as she carefully colored my lips. "You have loads of blonde hair. It just needs a bit of hairspray here and there." Dolores had tamed my unruly locks with her long fingers.

"I don't want to be popular," I had said, "I just want to be left alone."

"Okay, li'l sis. Whatever you say." Dolores had saluted and laughed her very Dolores-like laugh, head back and mouth opened wide.

I saw nothing funny. I never did. It wasn't a joke, it was the truth. I was happiest when alone. I didn't need people, for they just confused me.

The evening before she left forever, a ring at the door announced that Phil had arrived. He was always on time. Dolores sprayed a cloud of Anais into the air and twirled inside it like a ballerina on the top of my jewelry box.

"Gotta go, sis," she had said, kissing me on the forehead. "My chauffeur awaits."

I watched her leave from the window. As always, Phil opened the passenger door of his gold Ford Cortina and Dolores, curtsying and laughing, had slid her beautiful legs across the vinyl seats. That was the last time Phil saw her until the funeral where he placed the Paddington bear atop her white coffin.

I stared into that mirror and at that strange girl with the golden-blonde hair. The hairs that were fair and coarse underneath. The mascara wand on the dresser beckoned me. Gently touching the lashes from the roots to the tips, I darkened them until they were covered in gritty blackness. After propping Soft Mary on the windowsill, I stood back and smiled.

"How do I look? Is my hair getting darker?"

Soft Mary refused to answer. Instead, she stared at me with her turned-up nose.

"I think I've grown half an inch. What do you think, Mary? Are my legs as long as Dolores'?"

Again, Mary just stared at me with her one good eye made from an old bead and her mouth sewn shut. Taking the lipstick from off the dresser, I drew over my lips. I glanced outside and frowned. A plane had left a trail of white clouds across the darkening, violet sky. An angry gust was blowing against a layer of birch leaves. As they floated gracefully earthward, their colors were turning from a bright yellow to a darkening gold. A blanket of weariness was dropping and reminding me of the setting sun. Now I was falling out of the sky. My eyes wanted to sleep, to forget. My stomach ached. My stomach hurt a lot now that Dolores had left me alone.

I pulled Soft Mary toward the tightened knots of my stomach. Sometimes, Soft Mary would make the pain go away. But not tonight. I yanked off my brown-and-orange tank top and stretched out under the flowery covers. A flurry of images fluttered behind my closed eyes as I soaked in my sister's essence, stirring listlessly in an autumn breeze. A pumpkin with slits for eyes was puking seeds onto the pavement. Air was filled with smoke, and the jet black of leaves against the white roses mimicked the strands of Dolores' hair that blew across her pale face. Her eyes wide and blank.

I drifted for only a moment before the starless sky sucked me into the twirling darkness forever, dismissing the memories that lingered within my overly flawed judgment.

Lynn's thoughts …

What I liked about this short story is how the author entwined the idea of supernatural power into the events. I'm not sure if others will find what I did or not. However, the resentment the younger daughter felt toward the elder one definitely grabbed my interest.

Flawed judgement … the last words of the story. Did the child have misguided intentions or was it within her ability to control her environment? The idea of the younger resenting her elder sister kept haunting me. The younger never understood her sister's humor. She felt she was prettier than her. And so on and so on. Therefore, did the subliminal desire to be alone contribute to her sister's murder?

Then again, we could simply justify everything as a frightened young child hiding to protect herself.

I'm also wondering about the significance of the one shoe that was left behind. Is there a hidden message from the author with that one shoe? I used a single shoe to represent guilt in one my novels. In the end, does the second shoe reunite with the first to heal my character?

In this story, we never see the second shoe. Therefore, does that mean that the younger sister never heals? That she will forever carry the guilt of her sister's disappearance?

So many haunting, significant meanings are hidden between these lines.

PsyCHosis

Wilbur McKesson

ONE

"It's only for two days," Lauren said with her boots thumping across the hardwood floor. "I'll only be a couple hours away." She shrugged as she walked downstairs.

Elijah sighed. Once again, his wife was leaving for yet another company outing. He hated her boss. Every time Eli couldn't accompany his wife at job-related functions, Rick stepped in and took his place.

Rick owned a physical therapy clinic, which meant that his bank account was limitless. He constantly paid for weekend getaways, lavish dinners at five-star restaurants, and long nights at the most extravagant bars in town. That was how he rewarded his employees for their hard work and dedication.

Eli, however, was on the opposite end of the spectrum. He was a pilot who flew for Delta airlines. Since he was assigned to the international flights, he wasn't home much. Trying to raise two boys, Joseph and Kenneth, with both parents working seemed to place a heavy strain on their marriage. With all of this aside, Eli promised they could try for a third with the hope of it being a girl. The couple tried for the better portion of a year, but at the age of thirty-seven, Eli was beginning to wonder if he still had active swimmers in his tank.

"It's not the fact of you being away for the weekend, Lauren, it's –"

"*My boss?*" she asked. Wrapping her arms around his neck, she kissed him. "The kids are with my parents, so it'll be fine. Plus, you have all day tomorrow and Sunday to watch football with your friends. Which reminds me, did you send in the money for Joseph's trip?"

"Damn," Eli whispered. "I'll do that today."

Lauren stepped back. "You were supposed to take care of that Monday."

A loud honk and Eli opened the front door. He reached down to grab her bags, but she had beaten him to it.

"I'll take care of it," he said. "I had to train new pilots in the simulator this week, which makes the days longer."

She closed her eyes and took in a deep breath. Glancing out at the waving driver, she shrugged. It was Rick, her boss. A couple of passengers yelled out the windows for her to hurry up.

"You always forget things," she said, staring at her husband. "I've reminded you numerous times. Tell you what … you explain it to your son why he won't be able to see his favorite animals next week with the rest of his friends."

Eli leaned forward to give her a kiss, but she dodged and stepped onto the porch. "Lauren!" he yelled as she ran to the idling SUV.

Lauren didn't turn around. She placed her bags in the back and crawled onto the backseat. She waved goodbye and her boss peeled off down the street.

TWO

Eli grabbed a beer and sighed. It was Friday and the kids and his wife were gone. The house was his. Tomorrow and Sunday, his friends would show for the afternoon football games. As much as he wanted to start the weekend early, mentally, he just wasn't there.

Falling into his leather recliner, maybe a quick nap would lighten his mood. With a looming headache, he groaned as he settled in. But the pounding refused to stop. He urged himself out of the chair and aimed for the medicine cabinet. Gulping down two Tylenols, he shuffled into the kitchen and grabbed some water. It wasn't the fact that Rick and Lauren were spending a great weekend together that caused him stress, nor the fact that he was reaching his limit trying to conceive. The straw that was breaking the camel's back was forgetting to make the deposit for his son to enjoy Tiger World.

Eli's son loved animals, particularly the exotic ones. He had marked it on his calendar over a month ago. But that was before whispers of layoffs circled through the crew lounge. The newest strain of the deadly virus was spreading throughout Southeast Asia and Europe, which were his biggest destinations. Delta airlines was paying close attention to the overseas virus and had conducted an emergency board meeting on Saturday. Emails were sent to the workforce, preparing staff for potential job cuts. He hadn't told Lauren yet. Quite frankly, nothing had really happened and wouldn't be decided until the weekend was over. Not knowing the full severity of the layoffs, he envisioned being cut and trying to make ends meet on his wife's salary alone.

He reclined and shifted his weight as he nestled deeper into the chair. Looking over at his phone, he thought about setting the timer but decided there was no need. Folding his arms across his chest, he took in a deep breath and tried to calm his mind as his world plunged into a dark abyss.

THREE

"Eli," Lauren asked, "would you like more dessert?"

"No, I'm fine, thanks, babe."

She stood, kissed his forehead, and aimed for the buffet line. Eyes from around the room landed on her. Her elegant and tight, red dress stretched seductively along her wavy hips. Her long, scarlet hair always caused men to steal a glance when their significant others weren't watching. Lauren was gorgeous and the dedication she gave to the gym showed. Her losing the baby weight after Kenneth was born was like nothing Eli had ever seen.

The couples sitting at the other tables were Lauren's co-workers. They seemed content ignoring the world and immersing themselves in company gossip. Rick stepped out of line and walked back to stand by Lauren.

Who did this guy think he is?

This was the first Christmas they'd spent together after moving to Charlotte. He knew his wife would never cheat on him. Afterall, she *was* the mother of his beautiful children. Nonetheless, he refused to watch anyone, especially *her* boss, place the moves on *his* wife. Her laughter, with Rick at her side, sent chills up his spine. When the man placed his hand on her shoulder, Eli's heart exploded. He stood and made his way to the restroom.

The nerve of that guy, trying to make her laugh and then touching her like that!

He took a few moments to relieve himself and counted while he waited. Still feeling furious, he took in a deeper breath. He had to calm down. After zipping up his pants, he stepped in front of the sink. He splashed water on his face and closed his eyes.

"It's okay, Eli," he whispered, "she can handle herself."

Is that what you think?

"Who said that?" He spun around and saw no one. He turned back to the mirror and stared at the image that was staring back.

You really think she can handle herself?

The creature had the same dark hair, the same light brown skin, and the same gray eyes, but this *thing* wore an evil and sinister grin.

"I'm talking to myself?" Eli sighed. "This isn't real. Gotta be the lighting in here. This is just a dream, and you need to wake up. I'm going to count to three, and this other person staring at you will be gone. It will be just me in here. Okay, here we go … one, two, three …"

He took in a deeper breath and opened his eyes. He was still staring at himself. However, no evil grin smiled back. Just a calm, cool, and nervous reflection of himself.

FOUR

Eli woke feeling drenched. He rubbed his eyes and yawned.

What a creepy dream.

Grabbing his phone, he scrolled through the missed notifications. A call from Lauren's parents about an hour ago, a few texts from a group chat with his friends about the plans for the weekend, and a missed text from Lauren saying that they had arrived safely. The clock above the stove was showing 5:13, it was almost dinner time.

Eli FaceTimed his children and talked to his in-laws, ignoring the constant back-and-forth group chat about what college team was going to win on Saturday. Afterward, he called Lauren.

No answer.

He shot her a quick text,

> Hey, sorry I didn't respond earlier, I crashed.
> Hope all is well.

"Hope all is well?" he said under his breath, standing up and walking into the kitchen. "She's probably just busy chatting with the rest of the girls. Hopefully not with Rick." He rummaged through the refrigerator and managed to throw together some leftovers from the lasagna he had made the night before. Placing his slice in the microwave, he set the timer and watched as the plate of assorted cheese and meat bubbled.

Remember when we cooked together? the voice in his head asked. *When was the last time?*

"Been a while," he said, answering the thought that rumbled through his head. "Damn you, Rick, why did you have to show so much interest to *my* wife at the Christmas party? There were other wives there."

Balancing the hot plate in one hand, he grabbed a beer with the other. He walked back to the recliner, sat everything on the small side table, and turned on the television to ESPN. The commentators were discussing their predictions about tomorrow's games. But they were hard to hear with the rattling that kept haunting his mind.

Who does Rick think he is? He's a nobody.

"Just because he has money, he thinks he's a hotshot?" he asked.

He twisted the bottle top. Taking a sip, the questions hit.

FIVE

Did she answer your text?

"No," he said. "Not yet."

Pity ... you know what that means? She's probably hanging out with —

"Shut it!" he yelled out. "Stop thinking like that. She can handle herself just fine. We have two kids." Eli stared at his empty bottle and wanted another. He walked to the kitchen, grabbed the last one, and tossed the empty bottle in the trash. He twisted the top and took a sip.

The sun was sinking behind the trees, and the alcohol was needed. He looked down the neck of his fresh bottle. Shrugging, he downed the rest in a couple gulps and tossed the empty glass into the trash. He checked his phone again.

"About damn time," he said, looking at the missed text he received from his wife.

She should have sent you one earlier while she was on the drive to the cabin. Not waiting until she arrived. Bet she was talking to Rick the entire time and ignoring you!

"I'll make her wait before I reply."

What did she say?

"Wondering what I was doing."

She didn't apologize for the way she treated you before she left?

"Nope."

Pity ...

He needed to calm down. Pushing his phone into his pocket, he grabbed his keys and jacket. He darted out the door. He slid into the car and pushed the ignition button. The Tesla hummed and the touchscreen lit.

Check her social media. You haven't done that yet.

He opened Instagram and read over her profile page. A new notification surrounded her picture, and he could feel his blood pressure rise.

"Of course she's going to post a story," he said. "She's having fun with her friends."

Stop making excuses for her!

He hesitated before clicking on the notification. It was a photo of Lauren having fun with friends at a Mexican restaurant.

"Not terrible," he said, convincing himself he was right all along. She was just having a good time. "I can text her back now."

`Hey, baby. I hope you're having fun! I love you!`

Satisfied with the text, he tossed the phone into the cup holder and opened the glovebox, revealing a semi-automatic Springfield Hellcat. Guns definitely weren't his specialty, however, the recent uptick in robberies around the area more than justified his want of a firearm. He closed the glovebox and backed out of the driveway.

The drive to the liquor store was just a mile away. State laws forbid the sale of soda inside liquor stores. He contemplated what to do. Purchase a bottle of whiskey to drink on the rocks or grab a chaser to go with it.

What are you doing?

"Deciding what to drink for tonight, leave me the *hell* alone."

Let me help. Adjust the mirror so I can get a better look at you before you go into the store.

He wasn't a big drinker, but the effects of both bottles of beer within five minutes of each other wasn't helping to calm his nerves. Reaching up, he adjusted the mirror and studied himself.

SIX

The evil, grinning face had returned. The mouth now revealed a chilling smile, and in conjunction with the crinkled nose and brows, it resembled something that was possessed.

You should drive up there, it said. *Tell her how you really feel.*

"Too far at night."

It's only two hours. You can make it in no time. Besides, you'll have a bottle of your choosing to keep you company.

"And what if I get pulled over? How do I explain that to Lauren?"

Don't worry about that! You'll be fine.

"She might be happy if I surprised her, right?"

Of course! Ooh, you should check the pistol one more time to make sure you have rounds in the –

"Stop!" He grabbed the gun and shoved it in his pocket. Closing his eyes, he shook his head. He glanced into the mirror and the figure had disappeared. He stepped out of the car and looked around.

"Hey! Eli," Travis said, stepping up to him. "How's things?"

"I'm fine. Just grabbing something for the weekend."

Travis stepped back and grinned. He pushed his wire-rimmed glasses farther up on his nose and squinted. "You okay?"

"What?" Eli snapped at the man. "I can't buy a drink for the weekend?"

"You just look –"

"Tired. I just look tired." Eli licked his lips, almost tasting the liquor.

"Yes, of course. I'll let you be. I have people coming over. Gotta return with beer. Have a good weekend." Travis lowered his gaze and scurried past.

Finally.

Feeling frustrated, Eli entered the store and walked over to the bourbons. His gaze wandered up and down the rows until it landed on what he was looking for. After grabbing the last bottle of Jefferson's Ocean from the top shelf, he made his way to the checkout counter.

"Don't bother bagging it," he said.

The twenty-something cashier shrugged. The mohawk hairdo and tattoos that covered her arms gave him reason to pause. She handed him the bottle with the receipt. Eli crumpled the receipt and tossed it in the trash on his way out.

SEVEN

Before we go … check her Instagram again.

"Screw that," Eli said, cracking open the bottle and taking a sip.

He glanced at his phone and frowned. No return text from his wife. Closing his eyes and letting the bourbon run its course through his body, he thought of all the unspeakable moves Lauren's boss was trying to pull. He pushed on her name and waited.

"Hey!" her familiar voice sent a warm wave all through him.

"Lauren? Did you get my text?" Eli sat his bottle on the passenger seat.

"Hold on." The sound of others talking and having fun filled his ear. "Sorry 'bout that. Had to step outside to hear you. We're goin' to some Irish pub next … how're you? Sorry I … I didn't give you a kiss before I left."

She's intoxicated …

"Yes, I know."

"Who … who're you talking to?" Lauren's slurred speech sent ripples of rage all through him.

"I'm not talking to anyone."

"Oh, okay."

"How's Rick?" He shifted the phone from his hand to his shoulder. He gripped the steering wheel and shook it.

"You're asking about Rick?"

"Yeah –"

"You know what, I needed this break. It's been a long, emotional year trying to get pregnant, and I just need this one weekend, and you won't trust me? Give it a break." She sighed a heavy sigh. "Have a good night." The call ended.

The nerve of her! To talk to you that way, and with everything you do for her!

He glanced into the rear-view mirror. The ambient light from the parking lot was enough for him to see what was staring back. The bags under his eyes were darker and puffier. The top buttons on his shirt were missing, and now what hair he had on his chest curled out, as if something evil were trying to escape. His luscious hair was no longer luscious and resembled a bird's nest. He wasn't there in person, but his thoughts were running into a dark tunnel that just might not have an end.

You need to go to her. Show that Rick guy that you're not to be messed with.

Taking another swig, he laughed. "Maybe you're right. Maybe someone should show him it's not nice to take out other men's wives. Especially for a mini vacation."

Let's go then … you know what you have to do.

Reaching into his pocket, his fingers wrapped around the pistol. "I love her too much to let some punk be all over her like that."

She's totally clueless. You know what you must do.

EIGHT

As his car raced up Highway 74, Eli's thoughts crossed through his mind, increasing his rage and disgust.

"It isn't fair." He wiped his eyes with the back of his hand. "Rick is enjoying my wife, and I can barely see her? Why does a man like that get all the money? He provides for all his workers and it's so easy for him. Now I have to rely on my wife to make the money. It isn't fair."

What would he do when he arrived? Was he going to shoot Rick and make his wife somehow apologize to him? Did that seem like the fair answer to his problems? And what about his kids? If they sent him to jail, then what? Life behind bars for shooting his wife's boss. He would become another homicide statistic, and his children would grow up without a father. Lauren would never take his children to see him if he were in prison. And, even if she did, regular visits would become old very quick.

Thirty minutes out of town, he made a right onto Interstate 40, which would take him straight to Asheville. He'd not heard from the voice ever since he left the liquor store. Quite frankly, it was quieter this way. Stealing a glance from the dark road that was populated with nothing but tall trees and mountains on either side, he reached over for the bourbon. He tried to concentrate on the interesting label to help him stay awake. He tossed the bottle onto the passenger seat.

Take a sip already! You bought it for a reason.

"It's you," he said. "I'm going to call Lauren in the morning and apologize. She's right. This is her one weekend to get away, and here I am with a gun trying to –"

Oh shut it already. You're making me sick.

Glancing into the rear-view, the dark shape was now talking to him from the backseat. His heart pounded and he swerved into the other lane, narrowly missing the oncoming car. He glanced into the back seat, but it was empty.

"Damn!" Eli shouted. "I have to stop this."

He licked his lips and rubbed his hands across the steering wheel. He couldn't take any more of this stupidity. He grabbed the bottle and nestled it between his legs. Squeezing his thighs, he opened it. Placing the bottle to his lips, his eyes focused on the flashing red-and-blue lights that were behind him.

NINE

"License and registration," the trooper said with his right hand resting on the grip of his Glock and his left flashing a light into Eli's face. Running the beam back and forth from the front seat to the back, the trooper searched for something.

Eli's hands shook. Reaching into his jacket for his wallet, he could feel the frame of the pistol. He froze.

"Easy, slow it down," the trooper said.

Pushing the gun out of his mind, Eli whispered, "Yes, of course, sorry, Officer." Pulling out his wallet, he handed his license to the man. Returning his right hand to the steering wheel to meet his left, he waited.

Just grab the gun and go!

"No," Eli said.

"Excuse me?" The trooper shined the beam into his face again.

"Sorry, sir. I'm just tired."

"You swerved back there. Pretty drastically, actually. Almost took out that sedan."

Eli took a deep breath and said, "I know. Scared the shit out of me. I'm tired and my mind's playing tricks."

The trooper didn't seem impressed. "You haven't been drinking, have you?"

Eli felt as if his veins were pumping, "Of course not. I'm just tired."

"Where are you headed?"

"Asheville, sir," Eli said, feeling a little more confident.

Doing one last glance with his flashlight, the trooper handed back the license and registration. Eli set the wallet and cards in the cup holder and replaced his hands on the wheel.

"I'm going to cut you a break. My shift's almost up, and I don't feel like doing the paperwork. I don't smell alcohol, but you look like crap. Get some rest. Be careful and pay attention to the road. It's getting late and you're still about an hour out." The officer tipped his hat.

"Yes, sir," Eli replied. "Will do. Sorry again. I'll do my best to pay attention. I'll pull off at the next exit and grab an energy drink or coffee."

"Maybe you should do that," the trooper said. "Let me pull into the lane behind you. Don't need anyone rear ending you. Have a good rest of your night." The officer returned to his cruiser.

Eli sighed and smiled. He glanced at the passenger seat and the bourbon was gone. Not wanting to risk looking for it, he loosened his grip on the wheel. A cold breeze blew through the window. He rolled it up and waited for the officer to pull out. Now would be a good time to turn around. This may be the only warning he would receive for the rest of the night ... or his life.

TEN

Being pulled over was scary enough to keep him awake for the remainder of the drive. Entering the outskirts of the small city, he reached for the bottle and took a swig. Once the liquid touched his lips, he felt rejuvenated. Like a shock to the heart from a defibrillator.

I'm not an alcoholic, so why do I feel so refreshed?

The house was nestled in a quaint neighborhood that was off the main road. Before he pulled into the Airbnb, he took swig after swig. The golden liquid flowed down smoothly.

Two vehicles were parked in the driveway. The lights were on, and through the closed curtains, shadows were dancing around. Whatever they were doing, they were having the time of their lives, which meant –

Which means ... Lauren is having the time of her life with ... Rick!

"No, it doesn't," Eli stated.

Yes, it does! You're already here! You drove two hours to get here, lied to a police officer, and are sitting with a pistol in your pocket. How do you think the bottle conveniently disappeared? And reappeared when you needed it?

"What? What do you mean? It just rolled under the seat."

Bottles do not conveniently roll underneath seats by themselves.

"Well –"

Stop making excuses. Every second you waste sitting here, a second passes where your wife spends time with Rick!

"You're right!" Eli stated, stumbling out of the vehicle with the bottle in his hand. He knocked on the door and Rick answered.

"Elijah?" Rick said.

Two rounds sliced through Rick's chest and directly into his heart. Rick collapsed. A woman screamed.

Lauren dropped her glass and ran to the door. Her eyes darted between her husband and her boss. "Eli ... what have you done?" She ripped off her blouse and pressed it onto Rick's bleeding chest.

A woman ran up and checked for a pulse. She slowly shook her head and lowered her eyes.

"What?" Eli asked.

The ghostly figure that had haunted him from the back seat had manifested for only a moment. Eli dropped the gun and stared at it. As he did, the dark outline of a man's hand faded into the light.

"I'm pregnant!" she screamed.

Lynn's thoughts …

Wow, this one will bring on the nightmares for sure. Imagine being married to this guy? Talk about no trust … this poor guy actually created an alter ego to help him murder someone. In many regards, this author reminds me of Edgar Allen Poe, who pretty much summed up life when he said, *"All that we see or seem, is but a dream within a dream."*

This character was anywhere but inside our reality.

Jealousy is generally explained as someone's thoughts or feelings of insecurity that dwell deep within themselves. That the individual pushes their fears and concerns onto their partner, which in turn, only exacerbates the problem.

For most, having a backseat passenger yell at us, and a passenger that wasn't there when we started driving, would probably make us jump from the vehicle. Not this fruitcake.

Oh shut it already. You're making me sick.

Glancing into the rear-view, the dark shape was now talking to him from the backseat.

And … he kept driving? Ouch …

Maybe this story was written to help us understand that living with our alter-ego probably is not a good idea. And maybe … just maybe … it is time to seek out a shrink.

REFLECTION of Another Life

Shannyn Stewart

There is a mystical quality to glass. When I peer through a window, the life on the other side seems to vibrate. At times, sunlight and shadows project a false facade. Imperfections concentrate the light in some areas and diffuse it in others, resulting in the appearance of ghostly images that reflect from another time, another place, another life …

On a Sunday afternoon in late September, a hasty promise dredged unwillingly from my lips that whisks me to the south side of Music City, Tennessee. As I turn onto Williamsburg Drive, I watch as the trees roll past in vibrant lollipop hues. The glare from a blue-and-white sign captures my attention, and I stomp on the brakes. A name in black letters, a name synonymous with real estate and luxury homes, awakens my curiosity. Who is this prominent limb from my family tree that was severed with my paternal branch years ago? And why is she venturing into my neck of the woods? Is today the day that divine providence destines for us to meet? I steer onto Hampton Court, seeking answers.

The house is an off-white, A-frame that was slapped onto a tiny tract of land. An oversized picture window is the dwelling's most notable feature. From the signage on the front lawn, the crisp, blue eyes and platinum blonde hair of my half-sister greet me. I park and take in a deep breath. My heels clomp as I walk up the sloping sidewalk. Tender shrubs guard the foundation of the otherwise-stucco exterior, with sparse tuffs of grass sprouting on the outstretched clay carpet. The stained front door creaks as I cautiously step into the living room. The scent of fresh paint awakens my senses. My footsteps echo in the vacant room. A voice from the kitchen is coming from a man with graying hair. He peers out from behind the doorframe.

"I'll be right with you," he says. "Why don't you have a look around?"

"Okay." I stroll down the narrow hallway. *Who was that elderly man? Is my sister even here today?*

The bedroom on my right feels cramped. Across the hall, the bathroom wallpaper induces a flashback to the flower-power days of the '60s. The plush carpet of the master bedroom at the end of the hall absorbs the stomping of my feet. At the bottom of the basement stairs, a hollow concrete room awaits. A humming and newer-looking furnace sits on raised bricks, and a pool of water is forming underneath.

I sprint up the stairs and retrace my steps back to the living room. Sunlight streams in through the picture window and illuminates the stone fireplace. I turn toward the kitchen, anticipating a meeting with my sister. Instead, a small-framed man sits patiently, awaiting my return. His upbeat voice greets me when I enter.

"How do you like the house?" he asks with a broad smile.

"Kinda small but cozy." I scan the room for my sister.

"I must apologize for not speaking with you earlier. Would you like to step outside and see the view? There's a spacious deck with a creek nearby."

"Sure," I reply.

He holds the storm door open.

"Thank you." I step outside and the scorching sun blinds me. I can feel the heat hitting my skin. A low gurgling of running water sounds enticing. I cross the deck and lean against the railing. Mounds of grass that's been bleached white by the sun rises above the creek. On the other side, a wall of trees stand guard, protecting the property line.

"Nice, isn't it?" he asks. "Do you live around here?"

"No. I live just outside of Nashville. I was on my way to visit my mother when I saw your sign advertising the open house and decided to stop. She lives on Williamsburg Drive, which parallels Hampton Court."

"I must apologize, but I'm filling in for my daughter."

My eyes widen and my heart skips.

"She had another engagement this afternoon. I enjoy helping out from time to time."

A twinge of excitement bursts through my veins as it dawns on me to whom I may be speaking. I clutch the railing for support. I peer into his large, brown eyes, which also reflect my own. Completely enthralled, I begin a mental comparison of this man's features to my own. He's short in stature with a Roman nose – thank goodness I didn't inherit his nose. His ramblings reveal a toothy smile with wayward teeth. Poor Laura inherited his teeth.

My heart gallops into a tachycardic rhythm as I recall the faded black-and-white photo of a young soldier wearing an MP armband. Written in blue ink on the back were the words ...

Be sweet little daughter.
Love always, Daddy.

The man's features align perfectly with those of my daddy, only enhanced with streaks of graying hair and tiny wrinkles around his eyes.

"Do you have a family?" he asks.

"Yes, I'm married with two children. A son who's two and a daughter who's six months."

"Perhaps your husband would like to see the house."

"I don't think he'd appreciate living so close to his in-laws." I laugh.

A click from the outside condenser drowns out his soft-spoken voice, and we soak up the view in silence. Sweat shimmers on my bare arms, and I take in a deep breath.

Crossing to the opposite end of the rail, he sighs. "The weather's been quite hot for September."

"Yes, I'm ready for a cool-down period."

Silence follows, punctuated by the chirping of a nearby cardinal. The water gurgles and my eyes follow the current. Meandering along the property's edge, the rushing flow envelops any obstacles in its path. I was once told that a creek is actually a river's life blood. From the corner of my eyes, I steal a glimpse at the creek of my life blood.

Thirty-one summers have passed since I spied my father from a hospital bed. Through the blurred eyes of a six-year-old, I had glimpsed his hovering silhouette. "How are you feeling?" my daddy had whispered to me. My throat ached when I tried to talk, and I sank back into a drug-induced slumber. My daddy's absence was noted in many small ways. No birthday cards, an empty Christmas morning, and graduation and wedding announcements left unanswered.

But this is my father standing next to me.

My head throbs as my mind debates on what to do. Should I reveal myself to him or not? Bathed in the warmth of my father's company, I could simply stand beside him all afternoon. However, my mother anticipates my arrival. Not to mention, my husband will soon want relief from our children.

"I must be going," I state.

"Let me give you my card." He politely holds the storm door while I glide into the coolness of the tidy kitchen. From a nearby counter, he selects a card and a spec sheet and hands them to me. I slide them into my purse.

"By the way, I failed to introduce myself." He steps forward and extends his hand. "I'm Vincent Myers."

Firmly grasping his hand, I shake it. "I'm your daughter, Shannyn Myers Stewart."

His eyes widen and his mouth gapes open. He releases my hand and steps back, bumping into the counter. Our eyes remain locked, piercing deeply into each other's soul. He turns and retreats to the farthest side of the room. He stares at me and shakes his head. Leaning against the kitchen sink, he crosses his arms and legs.

"My daughter?"

"Yes."

"How do I know you're my daughter?"

"My mother is Gayle Sinclair, and I have an older sister named Laura."

"Why are you here?"

"I didn't know you would be," I reply, fighting to hold my voice steady. "Came to see my sister."

"Has your mother told you why I haven't had any contact with you? Has she told you the whole story?" He places his hands on the counter. "You should ask her what happened. I was stationed overseas. What has she told you about me?"

"She's never mentioned you," I whisper.

"My family doesn't agree with what she did and wants no part in your lives. If I have any communication with you, I risk losing them." He crosses to a high-back chair, fumbles inside his jacket, and pulls out a Gucci wallet. He thumbs through his photos. Tenderly, he touches a picture before handing it to me. It's of an attractive blonde with crimson lips.

"I couldn't bear to lose her," he says. "To think … she's so lovely." He slides out my half-sister's picture from underneath. "I'm proud of Jolene and her accomplishments. She graduated summa cum laude from Vanderbilt University and was valedictorian in high school."

Shaking, I sigh. "Your other daughters are doing quite well too."

The front door creaks and heavy footsteps echo through the room.

"Hello?" it's a man's voice.

"Stay here," he states. "I'll be right back."

"Am I too late?" a man asks. "Are you getting ready to close?"

"No, not at all. Let me show you around."

Their voices fade as they walk down the hallway. I seek the quiet sanctity in front of the picture window. Alone with my thoughts, I peer through the spacious glass. The mid-afternoon sun warms and relaxes me as the red leaves of a nearby maple rustle from an untold breeze. Peering through the glass, I can see images of a teenage couple. Both are dressed in their Sunday best and drunk from the giddiness of young love. Their kisses are frequent and deep, and when they come up for air, they share a smile. The young man races to open the passenger door for his auburn-haired beauty. The car's ebony exterior and chrome are polished to their highest sheen. Once seated, he pulls her closer beside him and they whisk off for South Carolina. The image fades as they travel the foreign roads in the dawn's early light.

Another image unfolds and the young couple is standing together in a quaint country chapel before an elderly justice of the peace. The groom professes his eternal love in a low and quivering voice. His bride pronounces hers interspersed with giggles. A steamy kiss seals their promise, and they hastily sign their names, witnessed by Ed and Gussie Smith. Seeking to satisfy heightened desires, their first night is spent in a small bed and breakfast near the chapel. The next morning, while dressing for breakfast, an old picture tucked in the back of their closet captures the young bride's attention. It's a painting on glass depicting a cozy cottage snuggled inside a dense wood. Smoke streams from its chimney and the mother-of-pearl windows adorn its exterior. She's taken with the painting that the owner gifts as a wedding present, and the gift still adorns her living room wall, even to this very day.

"I appreciate you showing me around," the man says. "I'll be sure to call your daughter tomorrow."

"Not a problem. That's what we're here for."

Their voices cause the images to fade and the rustling leaves to calm. Even though the men are talking in the same room, my eyes seek out the remnants of the ghostly images in the glass. The front door opens before creaking shut. Soft footsteps draw near and stop. His deep stare burns deeply into my back. My mind reels.

Take a long look. You may never see your daughter again!

Seconds slip by before he clears his throat. "How's your mother?"

"She's well and happily married." Encouraged by his softened tone, I turn and face him.

"Your grandmother was the sweetest woman I've ever known," he says. "Your grandfather told me of a trick he had played on her. Looking out of their front window, he exclaimed, 'Momma, there's a hippopotamus in the front yard. Come look. See for yourself.' Stella said that it was impossible and that she wasn't born yesterday. When your grandfather left the room, sure enough, she snuck a peek out the window. Your grandfather caught her and teased her about that hippopotamus for years."

I laugh.

"It's getting late," he says. "My family's expecting me."

I am your family too, my voice shouts out from inside my head.

He crosses to the front door and I follow. He turns, steps forward, and embraces me. I hesitate before snuggling deeply into his arms. My heart pounds as I rest my head against his chest. The familiar touch transports me back in time … to a place that my soul still calls home. He loosens his grip and steps back.

"When will I see you again?" I ask.

"I don't know."

Inside the loud silence, a haunting memory awakens. He had visited my grandmother at the funeral home. It was prior to the arrival of my immediate family. My finger had traced the curvatures of his name, which he inscribed in my grandmother's memory book. I actually mourned two losses that day.

"The next time I see you," I whisper, "I'd prefer it if you were not in a box."

He somberly opens the heavy door. I step out and fight to focus on my own obligations. Behind me, I hear a creak and a lock click. The sound seals the space that separates our worlds. I hurry down the sidewalk and open my car's door. I drop onto the front seat and search for my sunglasses. Glancing into my rearview mirror, an apparition of my father watching from the picture window tugs at my emotions. His eyes look moist, and his cheeks are glistening.

"Now … our faces look the same."

Lynn's thoughts …

There is so much to this story that I am not sure where to start. How can a parent walk away from a child? Something I have a difficult time understanding. Although, I understand that it happens and happens frequently. Half-sisters. The father accepts one but not the other two.

Inside the loud silence, a haunting memory awakens.

What a painful statement. How many times does a memory suddenly awaken from some dusty closet and attacks? It's a horrendous feeling. This man actually visited her grandmother's funeral, but before her family arrived. Talk about sneaking around.

I actually mourned two losses that day.

Another powerful and painful statement. Children remain children forever. When it comes to our parents, we never grow up. We look at our parents as parents throughout our life, and we always remain small in their eyes.

So … what do we do? Attack the situation or grow from it? Our character in this story seems to be growing and she is learning. But learning what?

Now … our faces look the same.

An excellent ending. In this last line, the author sums up that everyone is hurt under these circumstances.

Silence Redfield

Emily Osborn

The awful man was resting. The rhythmic thudding of the axe had ceased, and the slanted sun was at the precise angle required for his mid-afternoon slumber. In nigh a moment, Verity would bring out the stone jug of beer from the cellar. Her smug expression as she served would announce that she found the ritual, not only rewarding, but her path to salvation.

I did not see it so.

As was my custom during John Stafford's afternoon repose, I tucked myself into the byre, casting loose hay over myself. I had mastered the art of stillness in this exact spot and could remain without betraying my location. As was customary, I pressed my eyes to the slats of the byre and watched Verity crane her crooked neck, trying to spy me.

She lugged the empty jug and hissed out, "Silence! Silence! Thou art idle, I see it!"

I knew John Stafford was leaning against the oak tree with his hat pulled low over his brow. I waited until Verity had disappeared into the house, muttering to herself, before I slipped out to hurry across the open yard toward the old oak.

The master of the house was lying between the two great roots with his fingers interlaced across his belly. For a moment, I waited to see if he would sense my presence. When he refused to stir, I nudged his boot with my foot.

No response.

I nudged harder.

He grunted but slept on.

Feeling the devil dance against my nerves, I delivered a small, sharp kick with the toe of my boot to his left calf.

He roused immediately. Struggling to sit upright, he pushed his hat back on his head and squinted up. "Silence, what ails thee?" he asked in a fatherly tone, damn him.

I stared at him, my shadow thrown across his face in long lines. "I am with child."

John Stafford had the conscience to look ashamed for just the span of an eye blink. His features then shifted into the pious look of gravity that he wore on Sundays and for town meetings. "What wilt thou do? 'Tis a child doomed for hellfire."

Odd that in that moment, I noticed the first breeze of autumn had tickled the back of my neck. The ripe scent of the summer grass was supplanted by the crisp tang of the evergreens that ringed John Stafford's homestead. Strange that in that precise moment, I felt in my very soul that summer had ended. Running a blade of switchgrass through my fingers, I studied the man who held a coldness and distance that I never felt before.

"What can be done, John Stafford?" I asked. "I will bear my daughter into this world and live a life of isolation."

"Aye." He rubbed a dirty finger across his lips. "And know that I shall not abandon thee."

"Abandon me?" A musical laugh, a woman's laugh and not my usual childlike titter, bubbled out from my throat. "No, John

Stafford, thou art a good man. It was mine own wickedness that brought me hence."

"God knows that thou art not to blame for thy mother's evil nature." He nodded.

The reddening sun of early evening made his cheeks look rosy and his hair golden. In this light, had I not known him for what he was, I could have seen the good man that our community mistook him for. Smiling, I reached forth with my wisp of switchgrass and tickled John Stafford's nose. He made a face halfway between a grimace and a smile and brushed the stalk away.

With all the conviction of a frightened rabbit, he spoke. "And when the elders demand to know who be the father?"

"Why, the devil himself, of course."

Despite the rosy touch of the sun, the color drained from John Stafford's face. "Do not speak such, Silence, not even in jest."

"I do not jest." My tone seemed to physically press him back against the tree he leant against. "You said yourself, God knows my mother wert evil. Yet it cannot be denied that I am the seed of her womb."

He fell silent and his watery eyes glared up at me. Again, the devil whispered in my ear, and I found a malicious enjoyment in drawing out the moments that stretched between us.

"Does thou know what my mother's last words to me were?"

John Stafford's gaze lowered, as if I had uttered a profanity. He shook his head.

"I will tell thee," I said. "I remember them clearly." Another devilish pause. "With the noose already about her neck, she stared down at me. She stared at me so fiercely."

As I spoke, I felt myself return to that hill on that bright winter morning six years ago. My mother's face, the shouts of the rabble around me sounding faint, and my blunted memory. Aware of nothing else, I watched as my mother's lips moved. I could not have heard her, but her voice echoed deeply through my head as clear as the pealing of a bell.

"'Be not a slave of the righteous.'"

As I spoke those words to the foul man that sat in the dirt before me, I felt my spirit lift and shuck itself of his stain. As I towered before him, whispers and echoes danced through my ears. I felt an absolution, a decree of action laid across my shoulders by an otherworldly force.

As the final bloody rays of the setting sun sank beyond the forest, I drew John Stafford's axe from the stump where its blade was embedded. I inhaled the autumnal twilight while shadows lengthened around me.

Lynn's thoughts …

Another murder. How many does it make in this anthology now? I lost count.

What I enjoyed from this story is the author's goal to remind us that, although technology may change, how we live and how our emotions vary remain the same. Unwanted pregnancies are a normal course of life and have been since the beginning of time.

Have we, as women, learned anything? Absolutely not. We continue to fall for men who cannot fall for us. Oh, they tell us how much they care or love us, but in the end, *adiós amigo.*

As I read this story, I could see the young slave existing on a plantation and being used and abused by the master of the house. Something that happened quite frequently back then and probably continues to this day in some form or fashion. But I think this character found her just reward with the axe.

I felt an absolution, a decree of action laid across my shoulders by an otherworldly force.

Perhaps this is her inner self protecting her … straddling the ground that is crisscrossed with good intentions and poor judgement. Throughout this story, the reader can definitely become the young and troubled girl. I could see through her eyes and feel through her fears. Although short, this story is haunting and daunting at the same time.

Talons

Drury Wellford

Susan gently brushed a contouring dab of white onto the canvas. Leaning back, she studied the seashell she'd been working on for months. It was a humpback cowrie she had found on the beach the previous summer, and the dappling black-and-brown with a white underside inspired her to replicate it in oil. The dark, contrasting hues were a challenge, and experimenting with the various shades for the background was exciting.

She opened a bottle of linseed oil and turned it upside down just long enough for a sufficient amount to soak into the rag. Replacing the cap, she was careful not to damage her newly manicured fingernails.

Virgil, her husband, had remarked that her fingernails looked like the bloodied talons of a hawk. He often made such remarks to push her off balance. Her fingernails defined her status, and she wanted them to be noticeable. Once a week, she spent her time at the same manicurist who knew exactly how to shape them into perfect points and to only use the gleaming ruby red that matched her lipstick.

She glanced down at the smudges on her smock. The sight of the paint signaled chaos, her worst enemy. She'd have to hand it off immediately to Marybelle for washing. Every element of her life had to remain orderly and controlled. It was the only way she knew how to function, to give herself a sense of connection, an appearance of caring to the outside world.

She inserted an unfiltered Old Gold into the long cigarette holder. She admired the way Princess Margaret Rose of England communicated through her holder. It was elegantly to the point and an effective way to demonstrate a mood without using facial expression. If anyone ever bothered the princess, the cigarette holder would let them know. Susan wanted her moods to be communicated just as powerfully.

She lit the cigarette using her favorite Tiffany silver lighter. Smoking helped her control the twitching that taunted her when she was thinking or brooding. Inhaling the burning, bitter taste switched her focus from swinging her crossed leg, or clenching her fist, or staring at people. She took another puff and stepped back to look at her painting again. She was pleased with how it had turned out. It would be included in the showing she was hosting in her back garden the coming weekend. She might even sell one, although she certainly did not need the money.

She covered the canvas with a loose cotton cloth and left it to dry. As she was locking the door to her second-story studio, she looked over at Marybelle who was polishing the banister.

Handing her the paint-smudged smock, Susan said, "I'll be going to the dressmaker's and then for a luncheon at the Ladies' Auxiliary with Mrs. Carroll and Mrs. Taylor. We'll probably do a little shopping after."

"Yes, ma'am," Marybelle replied. "Do you want Master Bunny to have some lunch?"

"A peanut butter and jelly sandwich with no crust and a glass of milk may be brought to his room," Susan answered. "Remember, he is not to leave his room at all today. He must always stay in his room on Helga's days off. You have enough to do with minding the baby and keeping up with the housework, so Helga will clean his room when she returns tomorrow." She gave Marybelle a cold stare of rebuke. "Clara does the cooking and Helga is the governess. You are only to clean the house and watch the baby when Helga is gone. Is that understood?"

"Yes, ma'am," Marybelle replied, turning back to her polishing.

As she changed into her going-out Dior sheath dress, Susan thought about Bunny. Her oldest child was a problem. Out of control, violent, belligerent. Only Helga could soothe him. As far as she was concerned, the only person he could be with for any length of time was Helga. Helga had been her governess as well, and she had confidence in her. When Nurse Alma left six weeks after Bunny was born, Helga cared for him exclusively. Nobody else was allowed to even hold him. Allowing something like that might have thrown Bunny off his schedule. Now that Bunny was in nursery school three mornings a week, Helga would be spending more time with the new baby.

Susan's husband, Virgil, called Bunny by the family nickname for the Carrington men, *Virgie*. Her son, her husband, and her father-in-law all had the same name, Bunwell Virgil Carrington. Her father-in-law and husband had eventually progressed from Virgie to Virgil. They were now Big Virgil and Little Virgil. She rejected the idea that her son would follow the tradition and decided to call him by his first name, Bunwell. The Carringtons were unenthusiastic, but she stuck to her guns and went a step further by injecting a falsely affectionate twist to such an adult name, shortening Bunwell to Bunny. The nickname stuck amongst her friends and family, who felt they had no say in the matter. However, her husband's family continued to call her son Virgie.

Susan didn't understand the complication of multi-syllabic names strung out in a row. She had been christened Susan Will. Three solid syllables. No middle name, no baby name, no nickname. Just a strong, no-nonsense, orderly name.

She looked in the mirror, adding the finishing touches on the red lipstick she had applied to her tight, thin lips. She turned her head side-to-side to make sure her visit to the beauty salon the day before had remained successful. Not a hair out of place, and her hat looked stunning.

Satisfied, she picked up her handbag and gloves and went down the steps to the front hall before calling out that she was leaving.

"Yes, ma'am," they called back.

Once outside, she looked back at her historic house that her parents had gifted as a wedding present. It was charming yet orderly. Not a paint chip to be seen or a leaf out of place. Ordinarily on her afternoons out, she called a cab to go shopping at Hutzler Brothers. But today, she would be driving her black 1956 Continental Mark II, a gift from her husband. She and Virgil would be leaving the next week for a fourteen-day cruise down to Florida on her parents' yacht, and she needed to have an alteration done to her hostess gown for the art showing as well as a final fitting of her cruise ensemble.

Marybelle watched through the window as Susan's car pulled away before calling to Clara, "She's gone." Then she made her way up the back stairs to the locked door of Bunny's room. She knew where Susan kept the spare key while Helga was on her day off. She unlocked the room and slowly opened the door. She was struck by the odor of his feces and urine. Susan would not let Bunny out of his room to use the bathroom when Helga was off.

"Come on, Bunny," she called into the room. She could see him sitting on his bed, a book open on his lap. He was glowering at her. He slowly climbed down and walked toward the door, then ran past her and clambered down the back steps to the kitchen.

"Where's my lunch?" he barked at Clara. "Please, can I have a roast beef sandwich?"

"Your mumma said peanut butter and jelly today, Bunny."

"Don't call me that." Bunny scowled. He hated the baby name more than he hated the woman who had tried to make him that. The kids at nursery school teased him about it all the time, and when he insisted his name was Virgie, they teased him about that too. His last report card had noted his inability to play with others unless he was in charge, and his brawls with the other boys were continuous. His highest points were for punctuality and neatness. Unlike his classmates, he arrived at the school every morning with his clothes immaculately pressed, shirt buttoned to the very top around his neck, and his hair perfectly parted and combed down with water.

The bad report card had earned him a beating by his father, who came in that night when he was asleep, smelling of gin, and had woken him at his mother's insistence to punish him for his bad behavior.

"Why are you so hardheaded?" His father grunted as he slapped and punched him. Bunny had stopped crying a long time ago when this happened. He would never give either of his parents the satisfaction of knowing that he felt anything when his father hurt him. It was merely a test of wills between the three of them now.

"Sorry, honey, I can only give you peanut butter and jelly today," Clara said. "We must hurry. If your mumma finds out that we let you out of your room, if would be the end of us all."

"OOO-KAY," Bunny boomed and he started drumming the table with his hands as he chewed his sandwich and drank his milk, belched and snickered, and asked endless questions of the two women. When he had finished, Clara gave him some cookies, hoping that her kindness would somehow diminish his detached coldness. As he was finishing the treats, Clara asked him for a hug and a kiss. He would always give her and Marybelle a hug and a kiss when they asked. It seemed to be the only time he reacted to affection in any way that seemed normal. When his father tried to be affectionate, he stiffened like a board. His mother did the same when anybody tried to show her affection.

As Marybelle led Bunny to the back stairs to return to his confinement, the door to the kitchen swung open and Susan walked through.

"Marybelle, I forgot the hostess gown I'm taking for alterations. Did you hang it in the…?" And as she looked over at Marybelle and Bunny, her gaze hardened into a glare. She did not stop glaring until they had disappeared up the steps, and then she fixed her eyes upon Clara.

"Who let him out of his room?" Susan asked.

"Well, ma'am, Marybelle did, but…" Clara stammered.

"When she comes down, tell her to gather her things and go. She can return in the morning to pick up her final pay for the week."

"Yes, ma'am," Clara said.

Susan went into the living room and smoked a cigarette, being careful that the finished butt was neatly tamped out and removed from the elegant holder. Then she went upstairs.

As she gathered her things and slowly hugged Clara goodbye, Marybelle listened as Bunny screamed and pleaded with his mother who slammed his door. "No, Mother, please!" he cried. "I promise, I'll be good. I love you. Please, Mother, please!"

The day of the art showing came quickly, and with Marybelle gone, Susan needed to enlist Helga in the wild rush of preparations to make sure everything was perfect for when guests arrived. A punchbowl and tea sandwiches had been set up in the garden, while a bar and canapé-laden table were arranged in the dining room where the men could smoke.

Susan moved confidently among her guests, keeping a close eye on the ones who were looking at her paintings cleverly arranged around the perfect English boxwood knot design in her cozy, urban back garden. She felt slightly relaxed, having switched from punch to a sherry. She was looking forward to enjoying a cigarette in her room later. She knew her guests had admired her beautiful hostess gown altered to a perfect fit, its elegance enhanced by her perfectly styled hair and perfectly manicured and pointed red nails.

Helga and Clara had stayed busy making sure the sandwich and canapé platters stayed full, but now the party was winding down and it was time to clean the kitchen. Guests came to say goodbye, and Susan tolerated their hugs and kisses when she could not avoid them. One of Virgil's friends put his arm around her while Virgil filmed them on his home movie camera, and Susan spent the entire uncomfortable moment trying to get his arm off her. She despised slapstick hugging and joviality. She did not care how important this man might be in Virgil's office.

As the man pulled back from his attempt at friendliness, he looked up and said, "Hey, I think there's smoke coming from that upstairs window."

Susan turned and gasped. A smokey stream of vapor billowed out from her bedroom windows. Had she not tamped out one of her cigarettes? As she and Virgil ran into the house and up the stairs, she thought about what might be happening to her precious things. Would her clothes and furniture be ruined? She called to Helga to check on the baby and make sure Bunny was in his room.

She ran to the door and flung it open. Virgil stood behind her to take in what was happening.

Flames were moving up the right side of her immaculately made bed, with its damask bed skirt and silk sheets and eiderdown quilts. The bed was her haven, her escape from the world, and when she was in it she did not mind being touched.

She screamed as the fire moved rapidly across the bedding, and then …

Bunny stood at the side where the flames had already finished their work and the ashes were now smoldering. He had moved away from the heat and was watching the flames, a look of fascination was growing in his eyes. He held up the Tiffany silver lighter and smiled.

"Bunny!" Susan yelled.

He focused on her with an expressionless gaze of insincerity. "I didn't do this, Mother." He smiled and nodded. "Please don't get mad. I love you, Mother. It's not my fault. Marybelle did it."

Lynn's thoughts …

Throughout this story, I kept seeing shades of black and gray. What is the author trying to tell us? Then, there are the nails that are sharp as a hawk's. This character is ready to swoop down and grab her prey. And … the name … Virgil.

So much symbolism is in this story that if the reader doesn't slow down and examine every word, they'll miss it. Virgil means *staff* … hmm. Marybelle means *beautiful* … Old Gold, a symbol of *ancient wealth* … a reference to Tiffany that means *manifestation of God*. Wow, this woman is a powerful character. She rules through her husband (staff), is wealthy (Old Gold), is beautiful (Marybelle), and is as powerful as a god (Tiffany).

But in the end, her kingdom is purified by fire …

And purified by a child … the definition of absolute innocence.

She called her son Bunny. Meaning of Bunny … good, fair of face, charming, cute, and *he* started the fire with help from the hand of God (Tiffany).

Such a powerful and inspiring story. I would love to know if others found more than what I have.

The ART of Darkness

R. Aaron Falk

Grimilda slipped on a pair of pumps and checked her appearance in the entryway mirror. Getting older had not erased her little girl appearance. Something she used to her advantage on many occasions, but a pain at restaurants and bars when she was carded. Standing in the elevator, she watched as the numbers dropped from the penthouse to the lobby. A sweet scent of lilacs greeted her as the doors opened. She smiled, for the management always made sure there were fresh flowers in the entryway.

An elderly doorman wearing a dark blue uniform with gold trim greeted her. "Morning, Miss Grimilda. Thursday ... you must be after your mail."

"Morning, Jim." Grimilda smiled. She had few friends – by choice – and Jim was one. "Not that it matters much. All just junk on its way to the recycle bin. I only remove it so the mailman has room to add more. Keeps him employed."

"You've always been one to look after the working man."

Another resident entered and Jim rushed off to great them. Grimilda placed her key in her mailbox. She could have opened it with a quick splash of magic, but she avoided showing her skills around the Norms. It bothered her when they shied away or pestered her to fix things for them.

She turned the key and the mailbox opened. An odor of freshly sliced onions blasted her senses. When a searing flash of blue knocked her backward, her world faded into darkness.

Grimilda blinked once, twice, and tried to open her eyes. Something squeezed her arm and then relaxed with a slow hiss. Grimilda rallied her powers, ready to fight.

"Easy there, tiger," a familiar voice said.

"Peter?" She focused on the face that was peering down at her. "Where the hell am I?"

"You're in the hospital. Dr. Martin is taking care of you."

Grimilda glanced up at the cardiac monitor and frowned. "I don't understand. I'm never sick."

"You were thrown across the lobby. From the doorman's description, it appears that someone had placed a magic bomb in your mailbox. No broken bones, but a lot of bruising and a slight concussion."

Grimilda allowed his statement to seep into her groggy brain. *Had someone tried to kill me? Who and why?* "What do you mean by *appears*?"

"I checked your mailbox. The only magic residue is yours." Peter looked at his fingers. "Bit of a mystery."

"As the local paranormal investigator, then that's right up your alley."

Peter shrugged.

"Get me out of this place." Grimilda tugged at the blood pressure cuff that was still wrapped around her arm. "We're going on a hunt."

"You're going nowhere," Dr. Martin's voice said from the door.

"How are you going to stop me, Kathy?" Grimilda glared at the middle-aged woman wearing the white lab coat.

Kathy smiled and pointed at the talisman around her neck. "Peter suggested that you might be a problem."

Grimilda growled and glared at the two. The splash of concern across their faces gave her reason to pause.

"You have a slight concussion." Kathy logged into the room's computer. "We need to keep you under observation for at least twenty-four hours. Then, you'll be free to do all the hunting you want."

Peter held Grimilda's hand and gently squeezed it. "I'll do some hunting on my own. People don't do this kind of thing to my friends and get away with it."

"Be careful, Peter," Kathy said as he left the room.

They had exchanged a smile that made Grimilda clench and wish that Kathy was not wearing that amulet.

Grimilda poked at the rubbery, orange gelatin dessert that rested on her plate. She contemplated other uses for it besides throwing it in Kathy's face. A better thought would be to attack the idiot who invented the gooey stuff – animal extract mixed with sugar and artificial flavoring.

What were they thinking?

The wall clock clicked. She'd been sequestered in this bed since yesterday evening and needed to take action. But what action?

A knock and Peter's voice filled the room. "You decent?"

"Tell me what you found."

Peter limped into the room. Cotton cloth decorated his forehead and right cheek. The tail of a surgical thread poked out from the one on his cheek.

Grimilda sat up. "What in the hell happened to you?"

Peter sat next to her. His face looked tense, his muscles tied into knots. "You knew a source named Salice?"

Grimilda nodded and focused on the word *knew*. She held her breath.

"I needed a source to probe around the lobby and the mailbox."

Grimilda crossed her arms over her chest.

"We found nothing, so I persuaded Jim to let us into your apartment for a quick look around." Peter lowered his head. "The second we opened the door, we were hit with a blast of magic. Jim and I were behind Salice. I was cut a little and Jim broke an arm."

"And Salice?"

"She didn't make it."

Grimilda couldn't think. She'd only known Salice as a casual friend, but her death felt as if something had been pulled from her and thrown into a rubbish bin. A thought flashed through her mind. "A booby trap meant for me. It attacked the first magical source that opened the door."

"That was my thinking too, but ... the residue only had Salice's signature."

"No way. I mean, you're the expert here. But no one can make a bomb with a person's own magic, can they?"

"Not that I'm aware. Then again, I've seen things in the past that I believed to be impossible."

Grimilda wondered about the past events but remained quiet. "I will not just sit here and wait for whoever wants to kill me with my own magic."

"I agree with her, Peter." Kathy stood solemnly in the doorway. "We have no way to protect her here."

"Until we can sort this out, there's only one way to protect her." Peter searched inside his worn leather satchel and pulled out a bracelet.

"Oh, hell no!" Grimilda pulled back and slid her arms under the covers. "I am not letting you put that thing on me."

Grimilda stared through her apartment window at the dull, gray mist that was hovering just outside. Without her magic, her apartment seemed to echo the same image. She'd tried to argue against Peter's logic but to no avail. The only way to stop someone from using their own magic against them was to turn the magic off.

She examined the runes on the magic suppression bracelet. No one knew what the runes meant or who had created the bracelet. These bracelets had been around since before recorded history. She did, however, know of the effects all too well. No more magic until the bracelet was removed.

The doorbell rang.

Funny, Jim didn't announce anyone. Probably just bringing up a package.

Grimilda checked her hair in the mirror, placed a smile on her face, and opened the door.

Standing with only a slight hunch, a wrinkled old woman wearing a purple velvet dress stood quiet.

"Willowmina?" As the blood drained from her face, Grimilda pushed on the door. The harder she pushed, the less it moved. The door flung open, and she stumbled backward across the room.

"Is that any way to greet an old friend?" the woman asked, slamming the door behind her. She stood and looked around. "Nice place you have here. Nothing like the hovel where I live."

"You're supposed to be in jail," Grimilda said, standing up and brushing off her pants. "Where's your suppression bracelet?"

"It seems the worm has turned." Willowmina pointed at Grimilda's wrist. "Clever way to keep your own magic from attacking you. Although, it does leave you vulnerable."

"You took advantage of Norms, and they placed you in jail." Grimilda stepped deeper into her apartment. "Not me."

"Who cares about the Norms?" Willowmina took a step. "I'd still be free if you hadn't turned me in to the Guild. You're such a pathetic goody two shoes."

Grimilda needed to keep the old woman talking. "How did you escape?"

"The nice mage who gave me my bracelet visited weekly. He wanted me to see the error of my ways. I played along and eventually, he felt it was safe for me to have my magic back ... for a few hours each week." Willowmina sneered and took another a step. "I spent every minute pushing the spell at him. Just a little when he wasn't looking. Took me months to gain full control."

"He helped you escape, then?"

"He's my minion through and through. Does the nicest things for me."

"Like setting up magical feedback loops?"

"Clever, huh? Uses a person's own magic to kill them. I just make him invisible, and he touches you and sucks out your magic. Before you know what's happening, he sends it back in one big pulse. Boom." She threw her hands into the air.

"It didn't kill me the first time."

"He didn't hold on long enough. Practice makes perfect. Unfortunate that Salice came to investigate. The control and invisibility spells make my minion into a bit of a moron sometimes. Couldn't tell one *witch* from another."

Grimilda stiffened. "And what now?"

"You die." Willowmina cackled. "Without magic, of course. I thought about how. Perhaps slow and nasty with a touch of torture. But it'd be a bit more poetic if I killed you like a Norm." Willowmina pulled out a pistol from her handbag and pointed it at Grimilda, and an evil smile spread across her face.

"There's a flaw in your plan."

Willowmina tilted her head and frowned. "Trying to buy time?"

"Not really." Grimilda laughed. "The person who placed this bracelet on my wrist is the only one who can take it off. Why am I not trembling from your threats?"

"You should be!" Willowmina shook the gun.

Grimilda slipped off the bracelet and held it up. "Me?"

With her powers full, she raged and sent a magical bolt directly at Willowmina's wrist. The crack of bones breaking and the thud of the pistol echoed through the room.

Willowmina grabbed her arm and screamed out, "Get her, you fool!"

Footsteps pounded across the carpet. Grimilda searched for a way out. As a chair rose into the air, a loud scream echoed out and the chair crashed against a far wall.

"Two can play at the invisibility game, Willowmina."

"What are you talking about?" Willowmina asked.

"Say hello, Peter," Grimilda said. "He's my mage friend."

Peter re-appeared and stood over Willowmina, who was cowering on the floor. He nodded. "Time for you to sleep."

The sheriff arrived and slid a suppression bracelet onto Willowmina's wrist. The EMTs carried her minion mage and her away on stretchers.

"Do you think he'll recover?" Peter asked.

"From you tossing him across the room or from Willowmina's spell?" The sheriff grinned. "Dr. Martin will handle the physical effects. As for psychological or magical therapy? Hard to say."

"You'll at least change the rules about allowing unsupervised visits from persons who can place the suppression bracelets?" Grimilda asked.

"Goes without saying," the sheriff replied. "You took a damn risk." He rubbed his chin. "You should have called for backup."

Grimilda and Peter shared a glance as a slight wisp of white magic passed between them.

"Next time for sure," they said together.

Lynn's thoughts …

Always love a witch story, being called one on many an occasion. A witch on house arrest without magic? How sad, indeed.

A very enjoyable story with an interesting twist. At first, I wasn't sure what was happening. Although the name, Grimilda, should have been my first clue.

Overall, this was simply an enjoyable read. A comfortable read. And there is a lot to say about something that can take you away from the daily hustle of life. Even if only for a little while.

I think I enjoyed the names the most … Grimilda … Willowmina …

A little touch of Harry Potter during these turbulent times. I thank you for the enjoyment.

The Night Before

Tim Jarman

I want to make it quite plain that I never deceived her. She knew that I loved her, even though I never actually said it. And I did say it and more than once to myself. She loved me as a friend, full stop, end of sentence. Her message was always clear. Therefore, I was surprised to receive her text. It was nine in the evening.

```
- can I c u?
- Sure. Where?
- prince of wales asap?
- 20 mins
- be there x
```

The Prince of Wales was a gritty, little pub whose only virtue was that it was five minutes from her parents' house. She was sitting at a table next to the gas fire. It was raining and her hair was a little wet. She'd borrowed her dad's Mac, which made her look smaller and more vulnerable than usual. There was a gin and tonic in front of her. This was ominous.

"I thought you'd be busy," I said.

"I was. I am. I had to get out. It's a mad house."

"I can imagine."

I ordered a pint of whatever it was they sold and sat across from her. "Are you okay?"

The Night Before

She was wearing a lot of makeup, which wasn't normal. I thought I could see the beginnings of a black eye, but I wasn't sure enough to say anything.

"I don't think I can go through with this."

"Cold feet?" I asked. "Perfectly natural. Tomorrow you'll have forgotten all about it."

She looked me directly in the eyes, soul to soul. "If you tell me not to marry him, I'll call it off."

"The night before? Are you serious?"

She was.

My first thought was to say, "No, for God's sake don't marry him. Marry me!" Which, of course, was never going to happen. But what could I say? I never liked the man. He was to marry the only girl I'd ever loved, and because of him, I'd lose her forever. If he'd been the second coming of Jesus Christ, I'd still have hated him.

Did I have the right to say that to her? Didn't I want her to be happy? If he was the man she wanted, then she could have him. She should have him. If I was jealous and selfish and bitter, then that was my problem, not hers. I simply loved her too much to deprive her of what she wanted. I told her to go ahead.

"Thanks," she said. "I needed to hear that."

She kissed me on the cheek and left. Six months later she was dead.

I attended every day of the trial. I watched the man I had advised her to marry sit impassively in the dock. If he were even aware of my hatred, it washed over him like a breeze. His guilt was as clear as the sun in a pure blue sky.

When he was acquitted, I thought quite seriously about killing him. It would have been easy. I knew where he lived. I knew where he worked – reinstated, naturally, without a stain on his character. I knew the car he drove. It wouldn't have mattered if I'd been caught, so long as he was dead. I'd have turned myself in.

Instead, I accepted a job in another part of the country. I thought being a stranger would help. I hoped that time and distance might heal me. I was wrong. My hatred for that man ate into my soul like gangrene. I started drinking too much and eventually got myself fired.

I became sober and found a job as a porter in the local hospital. I was working the graveyard shift when the call came in – a big pile-up on the motorway, eleven casualties, three serious. All hands to the pump.

He was in the last ambulance to come in. They'd had to cut him out of the wreckage. I knew him at once, even before the paramedic started her recitation of his name and particulars. He didn't recognize me, of course. We were all masked up, and with the drugs he was on, he wouldn't have known his own mother. He was in a bad way. Suspected skull fracture, damage to cervical vertebrae, ribs caved in on one side, a punctured lung, and his leg was broken in at least two places. We added internal bleeding just for good measure.

I don't know how many surgeries they performed, but he was in theatre at least twice to my knowledge. There were plenty of things I could have done to him – turned off his oxygen, disconnected this tube or that. I did nothing. I expected him to die. It seemed like justice.

But he didn't die. He was placed on a regular ward. He spent time in physical therapy for his leg, and I'd push him there and back in a wheelchair. He never spoke a word to me, nor I to him. Then one day he wasn't there. Discharged. Healed.

I hit the bottle again after that, and my portering career came to an end. I was on the streets for a bit, and then I found a hostel. It wasn't grand, but it kept the rain off.

Most days I visited the public library and read through the local paper. The library was where I wrote down these words – on a notepad I had found in a bin, with a pencil that I stole from a newsagent. But I had to write this, because now I was free.

Today there was a paragraph at the bottom of page five of the local paper. Most people probably never even read it.

Local Man Found Hanged

Just his name, his age, the district where he lived, the neighbor who found him. There was no note. No need, not for me anyway.

There were two things I regretted in my life. The words I didn't say, and the murder I didn't commit. You could say that I had lost everything for love. But at least there was justice in the end, perhaps.

Lynn's thoughts …

We asked for stories with a little resentment, and I think this one captured it quite nicely. Courtly love entwined with murder. However lovely is that? Oh … and another murder in this anthology. I guess we all equate resentment with murder.

How wonderful is the taste of sweet revenge when we can sit back and just watch it happen? Our character struggles to deal with the death of his loved one and turns to the golden lady for comfort. Loses a job and walks the path of darkness. However, in the end, he reads the faithful words of retribution … Local Man Found Hanged …

I still wonder if the man hung himself or if our character helped a little?

… and the murder I didn't commit …

Not sure if I believe him or not. After all, no note was left behind and one wasn't needed.

They Liked Her Better

Jennifer Bukowiec

"Are you sure you don't want a lawyer?"

"I didn't do anything wrong."

"If you change your mind, just say so. Now, tell me what happened."

"It was only me for a while, then my cousin was born, but he didn't matter. We hardly ever saw him, so everyone still made me the center of attention. It was all for me, but she changed all that. I remember very clearly the day my parents sat me down and told me about her. I was almost five. A very important age in a child's life … five. I was about to start school. That was another big deal. Starting school is a milestone where your dad's supposed to take too many pictures and your mom's supposed to cry a lot, because you're growing up too fast. You're a big girl now. Ready to take on the world.

"'Rachel, you're going to be a big sister,' Mom had told me. I don't remember what my reaction was exactly, but it must not have been very good, cuz Dad got mad at me. 'Rachel! Stop it this instant!' He'd never yelled at me before. I knew in that exact moment that she'd be my parents' favorite. Every parent says they don't have a favorite child, but that's just a pack of lies that they tell their kids, so they don't get jealous. When you're not the favorite, it's glaringly obvious. My parents proved me right several times over."

"And how did they do that?"

"The first time, she hadn't even been born yet. They sent me to summer camp. Oh, they told me it was because Mom was sick and might lose the baby, but I knew better. They just wanted me out of the way. I cried and begged them not to send me, but they did anyway. She wasn't even out of the womb yet, and she was already screwing everything up, stealing all the attention. The next time they showed me how little I meant was more public. It was at my birthday party. They put *her* on the pony that they got for *my* party. My pony! My party! When she started to cry, Mom laughed and held her. That screaming baby stole all the attention away from me on my birthday. Stupid, ugly, smelly thing. I should've been the only person anyone even thought about on my birthday.

"It went on like that for years. My parents doting on her, and me getting into trouble for everything she did. She was a tattletale, always telling them whenever I pinched her. She deserved it. She was always saying something stupid or laughing too loud. She was so annoying that it set my teeth on edge every time she walked into a room. She even had the audacity to talk to me at school where other people could see. Just because we went to the same school didn't mean I would say hi to her in the hall. It was mortifying, having anyone know that we were even slightly related. I did the only appropriate thing. I ignored her. What did she do about it? Well, she didn't take the hint, that was for sure. She ran and told Mom and Dad. And I got in trouble, again. They gave some dumb speech about how I'm her big sister and need to look out for her at school, not pretend she didn't exist. Like I was going to do that."

"What happened after that?"

"I'm not stupid, Detective. I eventually figured it out. If I wanted something, I would simply convince her that she wanted it too. Then she'd ask Mom or Dad, and she'd get it cuz they liked her more. They never said no to her. It worked pretty good for a while. And then, she had to go and ruin that too. She told them that I told her to ask because I said that they liked her better. Who got in trouble? Not her for telling them our secrets. Nope. I got in trouble for lying. It wasn't a lie.

"It only got worse as I got older. Mom and Dad forced me to share a bed with her whenever we went on vacation. That's ridiculous. I was older and needed my privacy. I deserved my own bed. That's why I kicked her until she slept on the floor. That's where she belonged, on the floor. I was born first, and it was time that she respected that.

"I don't understand why everyone made such a big deal over the bruises. They eventually faded. But Mom and Dad forced me into therapy anyway. They said I had to deal with my issues. I don't have issues. They have issues. I never talked to the therapist. It was my parents who told the therapist what I knew already. That she was the favorite. The therapist tried to convince me to accept that. I refused. It really wasn't the major catastrophe they made it out to be. She was just being a brat. After that, I decided that if Mom and Dad liked her better, then I wouldn't go with them anymore. Who wants to go on boring vacations anyway? Not me. Not when I was about to start high school."

"High school was a big deal for you?"

"It is for everyone my age, Detective. High school meant a fresh start without her. At least, that's what I thought. Boy, was I ever wrong. Every time I had a friend over, she'd be there watching TV. She made sure she was there, so everyone would see her and pay attention to her. My friends always said the same thing. 'Rachel didn't tell me she had a sister.' It didn't matter! They were *my* friend, not *hers*. I got yelled at for it, and of course my friends included her in whatever we did. Even my friends liked her better.

"I'd had enough when my boyfriend told me to be nice to her. He was supposed to be on my side. I wasn't mean to her. I was honest about her. How dare he tell me to be nice to her when I was the only person to see her for what she really was? A stupid, ugly, smelly, fat bitch. I told her as often as I could. She couldn't change if no one ever told her what was wrong with her. That was when I decided to take my life back. I was going to reset everything, so everything would go back to normal. Just like it was before she was born."

"And how did you reset everything?"

"It was brilliant, actually. I announced that I was going swimming. And she always copied everything I did. She was such an attention hog that I couldn't do anything without her trying to take all the attention away from me. I put on my favorite bikini and went to the backyard. I've always had the body for a bikini. I nearly threw up at the sight of her in a bathing suit. I barely managed to keep my breakfast down as I dove gracefully in the pool, and she followed with some kind of belly flop. My mother praised her, naturally. I learned to properly dive years ago, and I'm good at it. That idiot was just learning, but her awful imitation of me was rewarded, and my talent was ignored. She splashed and flopped around like a demented fish. I bided my time until that perfect moment. Mom was reading, not paying attention. When her back was to me, I swam up behind her and grabbed her by the neck and pushed her under. I held her there. I pushed her down where she couldn't make any noise. By the time Mom looked up, it was too late."

"You drowned your sister?"

"Yes, Detective. What other option did I have? With her gone, I was an only child again. There was no one else to copy me or steal the attention away from me. No one will remember her. But they'll remember me. I'll be the one they'll like better again."

"Rachel, I'm arresting you for the murder of your sister. You have the right to remain silent. Anything you say can and will be used against you in a court of law. You have the right to an attorney. If you cannot afford an attorney, one will be appointed for you. Do you understand the rights I have just read?"

Lynn's thoughts …

Sibling rivalry taken a step too far? Takes us back to the days of Cain and Abel, the first to kill a sibling. There have been many murders in the name of siblinghood. Brother against brother … sister against sister. Makes me wonder if they were fighting before birth? Talk about carrying a grudge.

The whole story is from one point of view. The sister in pain. The other one's dead, so it doesn't matter what she's feeling. Not anymore. Writing in first person from only one point of view is never easy. We can only write what that character sees, tastes, feels, hears, etc. Anything else is irrelevant.

Stephen King wrote, *"Alone. Yes, that's the key word, the most awful word in the English tongue. Murder doesn't hold a candle to it and hell is only a poor synonym."*

This sister, although she lived in her family unit, was completely alone. The most painful state of mind to ever exist. A vacant emotion that rips out the soul and banishes it to the pits of an ever-evolving torment of misery. These people live a saddened and forlorn life. A singular trying to survive within the plural, something that just doesn't work. And this author captured it quite successfully.

They Liked Her Better

When Old Ladies Swear

Jeanne Hall

"Tanqueray and cola ... neat."

"And cola? That's a new one." The bartender chuckled.

"Are you going to pour that, or do I need to do a little dance first?" As her skinny shoulders spiked out from under her jacket, Agnes shimmied on the barstool.

"That can't taste very good." The bartender grimaced as she buffed the gin bottle til it shone.

"No limes ... no lemons ... no fruit." Agnes pointed at the bartender. "No shit."

"Got it." The bartender sprayed in the seltzer and the golden brew sparkled.

Agnes tossed a ten on the bar. "Keep the change."

"Just one?"

"Just starting." Agnes rolled her eyes and swallowed. She burped out a loud sigh. "You did good, kid."

"Thanks."

Agnes glanced at the singles floating on top of the twenty the bartender used to prime the tip jar. A quarter rattled somewhere on the bottom.

"I used to prime the pump too."

"Doesn't everybody?" The bartender winked. "Where you from?"

"Far away." Agnes clunked the empty glass on the bar. "Another? A little less cola this time, eh, sweetheart."

"I'm your sweetheart already?"

"By the look of things, you've been plenty of people's sweetheart."

"You're funny." The bartender frowned. "Really, where you from?"

"From out of town, visiting my kid." Agnes shrugged.

Her worn jacket was a size too big, but not big enough to hide her slender arms. Her gray curls waited for a reason to rise, and her face betrayed a life of squinting and smiling. Somewhere within the mahogany light, her eyes drifted over the unblemished bottles. She refused to look at her own reflection.

A customer entered and the rays of daylight and humming traffic followed them in. Voices now blended with the rhythmic mumbling of the jukebox, and the bartender's greeting penetrated past the garbage disposal of Agnes' hearing.

The gin seemed to loosen and warm her knees. Her heels latched onto the stool's rung while the spirit of the gin slithered up her thighs, climbing into her hips and into her spine.

"Ready for another?" The bartender held the bottle of Tanqueray.

"That's three, right?"

"Who's counting? Tell me about your kid. Got to be older than me. You look as old as my grandma. Why is an old lady in here and alone and before noon? Don't you have a soccer game or something?"

"Fuck no." Agnes smiled.

"I love it when old ladies swear." The bartender smiled. "On the house."

"If I say *fuck* again, do I get another one for free?"

"Fuck no." The bartender laughed ... her hair laughed as did her fake breasts. "When I'm old, I'm going to swear. You're now my role model."

"Be careful what you wish for, sweetheart." The gin sloshed the river of time through Agnes' head. Hard memories rolled around like stones in a stream. The old days bounced off, careening into lousy meals and a crying baby. The gin clogged the river as angry as the daughter that bounced against the wrecked car. A stone, once buried, whirled up and jammed against the emergency room doors ... sirens ... the static of a police radio from Santa Rosa to Amarillo now reverberated against the rushing dam and roared.

When she opened her eyes, the bartender was staring at her.

"Where'd you go? Have a nice visit?"

"I didn't have a fucking stroke, okay? Your music is horrible. I closed my eyes to tune out the band."

"Do you need better music or louder?" The bartender wiped down the counter and raised her brows. "Another?"

"You'll be wanting money, I guess."

"Money or a badass story."

"I have no badass stories." Agnes pulled another ten from her pocket. "I have no stories."

"I doubt that."

The door swung open.

"Mom?" A graphite silhouette stood in the glaring sun and leaned against the door.

"Shit … fuck." Agnes waved her hand at the bartender. "Don't bother pouring another. My ride's here." She tossed another ten onto the counter.

"Mom!" The woman held the door open with her foot. "What the hell? Again?"

The bartender placed her hands on the bar and leaned over. "Late for that soccer game?" she whispered.

"Something like that."

Lynn's thoughts …

The art of aging gracefully. Not something that everyone is capable of, but I think this character did a pretty good job. The best part of the story is when we hear …

"Mom!"

How many times have I heard that one? Not that I'm in a bar or anything similar, but it has the same affect. When did the roles change? When did *they* become the boss? I do not remember handing over the helm. Not yet.

The author choosing an older woman to demonstrate how life has a way of controlling us, especially as we age, was a good example. I guess we all have a *graphite silhouette* that takes control and makes us behave.

Darn … *something like that.*

They Liked Her Better
Page 223

Jennifer Bukowiec

Jennifer was born and raised a Jersey girl. She holds a bachelor's in English with an option in writing and a minor in criminal justice. She earned a master's degree in public administration and is a member of the Woodbridge Science Fiction and Fantasy Writers, as well as the Romance Writers of America.

When not writing, she enjoys cooking, baking, reading, or planning her next Halloween party. She has an addiction to tattoos by proudly wearing thirteen. She loves trying new foods and believes that all pets should be spoiled rotten just like her three cats, Pebble, Sprout, and Pixel.

R. Aaron Falk

The Art of Darkness
Page 207

Aaron is on his fourth career reincarnated. The first was academic physics, where he received a PhD from the University of Washington and a post-doctoral at the Joint Institute for Laboratory Astrophysics.

His second incarnation was in the Aerospace and Defense industry, mostly at the Boeing Company.

For his third incarnation, he started his own business, OptoMetrix, Inc., for the development and manufacture of test instruments for the semiconductor industry.

He is now semi-retired as a fiction writer and loving every minute.

Visit his website **www.raaronfalk.com**

Kathleen Fine

ID
Page 129
- 239 -

Kathleen received her master's in reading education from Towson University and an undergraduate at the University of Maryland in College Park. She's a member of the Maryland Writers Association and currently lives in Baltimore with her husband and three children.

She has written one novel, *Girl on Trial,* and has a blog at:
Instagram@kathleenfineauthor

Please visit her website to read more about her and her short stories:
https://www.kathleenfineauthor.com

Biographies

Tia Foisy

Absolution at the Diner
Page 33

Tia holds a Bachelor of Arts degree in law. She was born and raised in a small town in Northern Ontario and has written for as long as she can remember. Or at least for as long as she could hold a pencil. With a passion for performance poetry and short stories, she lives in the moment, being radically kind and creating stories and media that challenge others to step outside their emotional comfort zones.

Biographies

Mouth Sewn Shut
Page 151

Mary Fox

After leaving the hectic, rock-and-roll lifestyle surrounding her career in accountancy, Mary took a course in creative writing at City Lit in Holborn, London. Here, she was encouraged to write short stories. She has since been long- and short-listed in many competitions including *The Bath Short Story Award* and *The HG Wells Short Story Competition*. Her work is published in various anthologies including the Fish Anthology (2016), Trouble: The GRIST Anthology of Protest Short Stories, the Momaya Short Story Review (2020), and The Loop: An Anthology from Michael Terence Publishing.

She currently resides in Epsom, Surrey with her husband, two children, and a pair of hens named Tikka and Jalfrezi.

Biographies

Jeanne Hall

When Old Ladies Swear
Page 229

Jeanne is a single-syllable Jeanne. Her name rhymes with mean and green. She earned a bachelor's from SUNY Oneonta and a master's from Arizona State University, both in secondary education/English.

She currently lives in Phoenix, AZ with her gifted sweetheart and a legendary dog.

Biographies

A Very Unusual Day
Page 25

Rose Heaser

Rose is an award-winning author of nonfiction. She worked as a writer-director-performer for *Kid Biz* for twenty years, as well as nine years as a director and joint writer for *Crowder's Silver Follies*. She has directed the *Halo Benders* and the *Village Creatures Puppeteers*, as well as the *STIX Ministry* and *Children's Liturgy* for the *St. Canera Catholic Church*. She is a member of Joplin Writer's Guild. Her first book, *My Little Rosebud,* is currently at the editors.

Biographies

Lindsey Hobson

Home
Page 103

Lindsey is a writer from Southwest Missouri, where she lives with her husband and daughter. She enjoys writing across all genres and has been published in the adult fiction anthology, *Seasons of the Four States*, as well as having two published picture books, *Stop!* and *Blossom's Wish*. The latter of which was named *Best Children's Picture Book of 2020* by the Missouri Writers' Guild.

When not writing, you can find Lindsey at the local bookstore, adventuring in the Ozarks, or cheering for her daughter's softball team.

Do You Know Your Neighbors?
Page 63

How About Some Pie?
Page 115

Denise Israel

Denise's writing passion began two years ago when she retired from her practice as a clinical psychologist and was at odds with herself. She stumbled into a family tree with births and marriages that just didn't jive, and all from the 19th century.

With no one to turn to for her true family history, she decided to write a fictional account about the life of her great-grandmother, which has turned into a novella.

Now, she is hooked on storytelling and publishing stories. She is currently working on several novels.

Tim Jarman

The Night Before
Page 217

Tim has wanted to be a writer for as long as he can remember. He grew up in the West Midlands of England, which was during the post-industrial years before it became trendy.

After studying English at Oxford, he went on to write software for a living. This is his first story to be published, although, he has produced as a playwright and has given public readings of his poetry.

Nowadays, he lives in the wilds of Galicia, Spain with his wife, cat, and chickens, growing vegetables, drinking wine, and anticipating the end of the industrial civilization.

Biographies

Having Words
Page 95

Micaela Meder

Micaela is a twenty-five-year-old living in New Zealand. She started writing stories when she was around seven. Needing an outlet for her highly active imagination, writing became her passion. She is in her final year of study toward qualifying in early childhood education.

Her favorite aspects of writing – imagination, adventure, playfulness and self-expression – are echoed in the values she seeks to help protect and encourage through her work as an early childhood teacher.

Psychosis
Page 163

Wilbur McKesson

Wilbur has always had a creative mind with a passion for writing. Growing up in Southern California, he read Tom Clancy novels where he found his inspiration.

After graduating high school, Wilbur joined the U.S. Coast Guard, where he's served over twelve years of active duty in law enforcement.

Recently, he self-published an action-thriller novel, *Insertion*, and is currently editing the sequel.

He holds a bachelor's in criminal justice with a concentration in homeland security and a minor in psychology.

Biographies

Silence Redfield
Page 191

Emily Osborn

Emily is a writer originally from Michigan and currently living in the beautiful city of Chicago. She has spent the bulk of the pandemic working on her novel *Badass Women Astronauts on an Alien World* and perfecting her mezcal margarita.

She is an avid lover of folklore and mythology and draws inspiration from creatives such as Jeff VanderMeer, Kay Nielsen, and Catherynne Valente.

She is thrilled to have *Silence Redfield* included in Indignor House's annual anthology and hopes to contribute again in the future!

Biographies

Reflection of Another Life
Page 181

Shannyn Stewart

Shannyn grew up in the shadows of the Blue Ridge Mountains. An account representative by trade, her love of writing piqued during a summer program on international business at Magdalen College, University of Oxford.

Each day, Shannyn hastened past the medieval chapel to classes in the cloister, with its ornate stone arches, white hydrangeas, and bench-lined corridors, which she slowly found were calling her to write. On her last night at Magdalen, she dined in the candlelit dorm room of Oscar Wilde.

As she studied Wilde's life-size portrait, Shannyn began to envision this setting as the likely birthplace of Dorian Gray, even daring to imagine Oxford as the wellspring of her own characters someday. "Reflection of Another Life" is Shannyn's first short story, which was originally penned as the final exam for an introductory creative writing class at Salem College.

Biographies

Enlightenment
Page 81

Sue Ellen Russell

Sue Ellen graduated from the University of Virginia with a bachelor's in government, and then worked on Capitol Hill for Congressman Stanley Lundine (D.NY) and Senator Gary Hart (D.CO). Her federal experience reinforced her interest in the law, and she obtained her Juris Doctor from the Washington College of Law.

After graduation, she spent two decades pursuing justice for individuals and nonprofits appearing before Congress, other branches of the federal government, and those wronged by corporations.

Sue Ellen left her legal practice and continues her advocacy by writing fiction. She hopes she will engage readers and challenge them to empathize with individuals and issues that support human rights.

Sue Ellen lives with her husband and cat in Annapolis, Maryland.

Biographies

Just Like Daddy
Page 139

Frank Shima

As a native of New Prague, Minnesota, Frank either entertains or annoys his neighbors by playing Czech songs on his accordion.

He is a member of The Playwrights' Center and has written three novels, *Vencil, Dead Letter: A Murder Mystery,* and *Plum Creek.*

His plays have been performed throughout the United States in Alabama, California, Florida, Georgia, Long Island and Manhattan, New York, Louisiana, Massachusetts, Minnesota, North Carolina, as well as Ohio, and in England and Wales where he learned not to put regular gas in a diesel engine.

Biographies

Band of Gold
Page 39

Estevao "Steven" Sousa

Steven is a machinist living in rural Maine. He is surrounded by a large family of characters, wanderers, and adventurers. He's an aspiring writer without credentials or acclaim of any kind.

His greatest writing accomplishment is finishing his first, unpublished, novel.

Besides being a prolific reader and dedicated author, he's also an avid bowler, lover of billiards, pipe and cigar enthusiast, sports fanatic, wine aficionado, expert joke-teller, and generally an exemplary father.

A Father's Son
Page 7

Nick Tseffos

It was the world of *experience* that shaped Nick's life. He was the first person in his family to graduate from college. By age thirty-three, he became vice president of sales for a Fortune 500 company. He spent the next twenty years as a partner in a high-tech firm until he decided to pursue his lifelong passion for writing.

To hone his craft, he studied at The Loft in Minneapolis under the guidance of various authors. As a member of the International Thrill Writers, he was selected for Thriller-Tique, a pilot program providing virtual critique groups.

His short stories have won various awards, including some from The Mill in Appleton, WI.

His motto is, *"The world is never black and white ... it is gray. Our relationships weave through these lines, looking for stability. But our journey through the instability is what creates a great story."*

Drury Wellford

Good Neighbor Policy
Page 89

Talons
Page 197

Drury writes fiction, poetry, and creative non-fiction. Her work has appeared in the *Artemis Journal*, *Life in 10 Minutes*, and the Poetry Society of Virginia's Collected Poems of 2021, as well as *Quilted Poems: An Ekphrastic Collaboration of Poets and Quilters*.

She currently lives in her native city of Richmond, VA.

Biographies

Michelle Wheeler

Beggars Can't Be Choosers
Page 49

Cooked
Page 57

Michelle earned her master's in educational leadership, serving twenty years teaching grades K-8. She was recognized by the state of Florida as a high impact teacher. Her fascination with writing shorts was cultivated in childhood while reading works from her father's bookshelf, including those by Oliver Sachs, James Thurber, Fyodor Dostoevsky, and Anton Chekhov. These authors remain her greatest inspiration for creating absurd shorts with an underlying humor that can only come from total exasperation with the main characters' actions.

Michelle currently serves as the interim Executive Director of Laura (Riding) Jackson Foundation, a literary non-profit offering writing programs for teens and adults. She feels passionate about serving the literary needs within the community of Vero Beach. She belongs to Tuesday Writers, a literary group offering collaboration for published, self-published, and unpublished members.

Michelle spends her free time forcing her husband to read her writings and dragging her golden retriever through endless circles around their cul-de-sac. Especially when hashing out a new character.

Biographies

The Shoes
Page 3

Lynn Yvonne Moon

Lynn is an award-winning American author of over eleven novels. Her successful Agency Series for adults and young adult series, Journey's Travels, have won numerous, nation-wide awards.

She was born and raised in Ventura, California where she played on the sloping, tree-covered hills while watching military aircrafts zoom across the skies. After graduating with a master's in public administration, she worked for federal, state, and commercial companies under black ops programs.

Throughout her life, she has asked the harsh questions as to the *whys* and never has she been afraid to push for an answer.

Lynn is a graduate from Troy State and Lindenwood University. In 2020, Lynn and her editor, Shannon Pearson, and her mentor, Mark Lumer, established Indignor House to provide an avenue for new voices.

She is an avid reader, remedial editor, and loves gardening and playing with her grandchildren.

9 781953 278340